AGING GRACEFULLY TOGETHER

A Story of Love & Marriage

A Gift For : ______________________

From : ______________________

Date : ______________________

Also by
John Schlarbaum

The Doctor's Bag
A Sentimental Journey

AGING GRACEFULLY TOGETHER

A Story of Love & Marriage

SCANNER PUBLISHING
Windsor, Ontario
Canada

Canada Cataloguing in Publication

Schlarbaum, John, 1966 -
Aging Gracefully Together :
A Story of Love & Marriage
John Schlarbaum – 1st Edition

ISBN 0-9738498-1-9

I. Title.

PS8637.C448A64 2006
C813'.6 C2006-900007-7

SCANNER PUBLISHING
5060 Tecumseh Road East, Suite #1106
Windsor, Ontario, Canada N8T 1C1

Cover design:
Will and Jen Hawksworth © 2006
Printed in Canada

ACKNOWLEDGEMENT

One of my favourite films is "It's A Wonderful Life", in which James Stewart learns that a person who has friends can never be a failure. After publishing my first book *The Doctor's Bag* last year, I can attest to the above statement. Even before I sold a single copy, the support and encouragement I received from my friends – both old and new ones - and my family made me feel like a success from Day One. For that, I thank you all.

Dedication

For Cindy

- my original inspiration

For better or worse.

For richer or poorer.

In sickness and in health.

'Til death do us part.

- Traditional wedding vows

CHAPTER ONE

"The Unbroken Circle of Love"

****

Henry Cole opened his fridge door and peered inside, as the light from within, lit the otherwise dark kitchen area. His place wasn't much really. It was more like a bachelor pad, than a full sized apartment, but he'd called it home since starting college a year earlier. Ten feet away, sitting with her back to him, was Tina Gordon - a beautiful brunette who was watching television. Henry smiled as he reached into his pant's pocket to retrieve his most prized possession: a small blue jewellery box. Making sure Tina was still enthralled with her show, he ventured a look at the contents.

"This is it," he whispered to himself. "Tonight it's do or die."

"You better hurry up, Henry, this is getting really interesting," Tina yelled over her shoulder. "You just missed the best part. Spangler disguised himself as a cheerleader to get past the stadium security."

"I'm sure it is fascinating, but it isn't exactly Masterpiece Theatre."

"How can you say that? There's intrigue, conflict, and the climax, when Spangler is going to blowtorch that gym locker open. Then the entire nation will finally discover what Jim Haggarty has hiding in there."

Henry placed two sodas on the makeshift coffee table made of milk crates and a piece of formica before sitting beside Tina. "A big football superstar like Haggarty probably has the largest collection of panties that any men's locker room has ever seen!"

"That's disgusting!"

"And that's why Spangler is on the air."

As Tina continued to watch the program - the host was doing his best to slip out of his cheerleader uniform - Henry glanced over at his girlfriend of almost one year. They had first met by accident at the local beach. They had in reality grown up only a few miles apart, but attended different public and secondary schools. Neither would admit it was love at first sight, but both knew the truth. Maybe it was Henry's tight shorts and dark tan that caught Tina's eye (as well as a few of her friends). For Henry it undoubtably was Tina's striking beauty (her revealing swimsuit didn't hurt either). He had literally stumbled upon her as he tried to catch a frisbee. It was not the most graceful entrance ever, but it did get Tina's attention. After stammering out an appropriate apology, he impulsively asked if she would like to go for coffee. The rest, as they say, is history. Now with a year of college behind them, Henry was ready to ask some very important questions of Tina regarding their future.

"Don't you think there are more important things in life than watching these stupid exploitive television programs?"

"Yeah . . . like what?"

"How about marriage?" he ventured.

"How about it?"

Henry could instinctively tell this wasn't going to go as smoothly as he had hoped. "Well I was just wondering what your thoughts were on the subject?"

"You know my feelings." Tina turned her full attention from the TV to Henry. "It's a ridiculous pagan religious ritual, acted out by two very unstable people, who think they're *in love,* due to questionable ideals programmed into their minds by their parents and our uncaring society."

"What was the topic again?" Henry joked, shaking his head. "Thermal nuclear war or . . . yes, I can see it now . . . the topic was the sacred bond of marriage. And correct me if I'm wrong but I have a sneaky suspicion that you're against it. Am I right?"

"It's not that I'm against it per se," Tina started slowly. "I guess I just don't embrace the concept."

Henry couldn't believe what he was hearing. After months of scrimping and saving for this one evening, Tina was only now telling him what she really thought of getting hitched.

"But it's what makes the whole world go around!" he cried out exasperated. "It's the basis of our civilization. The genesis of the family unit: your family - my family - the Spencer's next door. Hey, even the Flintstones. Without Fred and Wilma and

Barney and Betty, there would be no Pebbles and Bam Bam."

"Don't forget Dino - he was always part of the family in my books," Tina said. "And while we're on this family topic - what about Mr. and Mrs. Hitler? Or the Manson family?"

"The Manson family doesn't count."

"Why not? They were a close-knit unit that loved each other."

"But it wasn't real love - it was an artificial love. A doped up kind of love. And as far as I know no one actually married Charlie."

Tina pulled her legs up under her bulky sweatshirt. "So you're saying that people can marry only if they have *true* feelings of love for one another?"

"Well I think it's a great asset," Henry replied.

"But when does a person know they're in love?" Tina responded combatively. "How long do you think it takes for a couple to realize that what they're feeling is love? Not infatuation, not I-really like-you-a-lot love, but this all-important-to-getting-married love you profess?"

Henry was taken aback by Tina's sudden aggressiveness. On one hand, he had always enjoyed debating with her on any subject, but tonight's showdown wasn't making an already nerve racking situation any easier.

"Well . . ." was all he could say before Tina continued her point.

"A year? Is that a good indication that you

know a person well enough to share the rest of your mortal life with? How about two years? Or five years? Or even ten years? Does anyone really know their spouse even after twenty years? Or is it that they just know what they'd do in certain predictable situations? Well?"

"I don't think the length of time you know a person really matters," Henry began in his defense. "But you should have a good basis on which to make a decision that will ultimately affect the rest of your life."

Unable to fathom how such a simple question like, *What are your thoughts on marriage?* could get so out of hand, Henry walked back into the kitchen. Tina, knowing she was winning this little argument, decided to up her attack.

"What about impulse or intuition? For that matter - fate? You hear all the time how two people bump into each other at a fast food restaurant on a Friday night and next thing you know, they're tying the knot Sunday afternoon! And most of these marriages last longer than ones where the people have been dating for years."

Tina stopped talking and gazed at the TV with a huge smile on her face. She could hear Henry rummaging in the fridge but didn't care to see what else he was doing. If she had turned around she would have seen him staring helplessly at the contents of that small blue box.

"I just have to keep my cool. She's just playing with my emotions," he said under his breath as he tried to reassure himself. Shutting the fridge door, he reluctantly returned to the war-zone empty handed.

"All this talk about knowing the person you're going to marry has got me thinking," Tina said as she made room on the couch for Henry to sit back down. "Now I've known you for almost twelve months, but I don't *really* know you. You know?"

"But would you say if the topic of engagement came up that you could make a decision based on our three hundred-plus days together?" Henry held his breath awaiting her answer. He didn't have to wait long.

"Who knows? And frankly who cares? The topic hasn't come up, but I know if it ever did, I'd probably say . . ." The sentence drifted off as Tina's train of thought seemed to temporarily derail.

"Well?"

"Well I don't know," she finally admitted. "There's a lot to consider."

"Like what?" Although he saw a small opening in her argument, Henry wasn't sure if he could crawl his way through it or not yet. "Do you think we should live together first? Or are you looking more at my financial records?"

The questions appeared to agitate Tina more than to suppress any misgivings she had. "I'm looking at everything, Henry, and you should too!" she instructed. "Who wants to marry poor? Can you name one married couple who didn't first consider their financial situation?"

"Sure," Henry said confidently. "My parents."

"Your parents don't count. That was thirty years ago - everyone was poor back then. Times change."

"But love doesn't." As reasoning with Tina by way of her head wasn't working, Henry quickly decided to gently pull on her heartstrings instead. "It has been around since the beginning of time with every person receiving and giving love at least once in their lifetime. We all know how it feels. It's that sensation my Mom and Dad felt walking down the aisle thirty years ago. Or that your cousin Margaret felt last year, when she got married."

"But," Tina interrupted his little speech, "when she got married she knew her financial situation was very sound."

Henry was astounded. "Are you saying Margaret wouldn't have married Tom if he wasn't loaded?"

"No, I'm not! She loves him very much and you know it. You're trying to put words in my mouth."

No, I'm trying to put this ring on your finger, Henry thought touching his pocket.

"But what if he was poor? Do you think they would have gotten married anyway?" He could tell this line of questioning was getting Tina more and more ticked off with him.

"I can't speak for her, but I doubt if she would have."

"Ah huh!" Henry proclaimed triumphantly. "So she married for money then? Not love, right?"

"You're impossible!" Tina leapt off the couch

and stomped into the kitchen in search of a snack in the refrigerator. "That's not what I meant, but it does help if you want to start a marriage off right. Haven't you heard that love doesn't pay the rent?"

"What about 'love conquers all'? I think once they're married, a poor couple in love can be just as fulfilled as any rich couple."

Tina returned from the kitchen with an apple in hand and slumped back onto the couch.

"But you said a few minutes ago that 'love is love'. Even I know that money doesn't always ensure happiness," Tina admitted. "No one - not your parents, not my parents - no one really knows if they love the person they share a bed, home, and family with."

"That's where you're wrong. If you are truly in love you know it. You're being too cynical."

"I'm right and you know it, Henry! I'll give you an example. When I was in the ninth grade I was totally in love with Hank Allen and he was in love with me. We were to get married right after high school graduation."

"That doesn't count. You were fourteen years old. It was puppy love."

"Okay, then what about when I was sixteen and Dwight Williams gave me a promise ring? That $60 ring was the most important thing in the whole world to me." Tina fell back into the cushions and looked to the heavens. "It was my destiny to be Tina Marie Williams," she said with a sigh.

"And how did Dwight view this ring?" Henry laughed.

"Probably the same as I did, until Eleanor Samples discovered there was more leg room in the back of a Chevy than in the front!"

Henry tried to control himself. "A case of simple infatuation."

"Didn't your mother ever tell you that if you think you are in love, then you are? The way you talk, at some certain age we all should be able to decide if the feelings we have for our boyfriend or girlfriend are real, or if they're just imagined. That's ludicrous. That's like saying by thirty everyone should have figured out Einstein's theory of relativity!"

"I think as we grow older we have a clearer way of thinking about certain subjects, that's all," Henry countered. "When I was younger the thought of marriage was stupid. Why tie yourself down when there were so many other fish in the sea? But . . . as I've matured the idea of marriage and having a family is very appealing."

"Under the right circumstances, of course."

"Well I guess you could . . ."

"You have to have a good job, some security and extra moola in the bank," Tina butted in. "Those kinds of circumstances?"

"I guess." At that moment Henry regretted his remark, knowing Tina would now utilize every trick she knew, to twist his words against him.

"Now what do those things have to do with marriage?" Tina jumped in, much to Henry's chagrin. "You've said your parents married for love - not money. So isn't the way they got married good enough for you today? Why should someone like me care if you're rich, as long as we love each other, right?"

"Okay, you got me on that one. Now I've got something to ask . . ." Although he desperately wanted to just pop the question then and there to get it over with, Tina wasn't about to let up on her assault.

"What about marrying just for money? Is there no hope that two people can fall in love *after* they tie the knot? And what about marriages of convenience? Or look at arranged marriages. Is the love these two share after being forced together any different from the love of two people who get married of their own free-will? Well?"

With each point Tina's voice had risen in pitch. As the seconds ticked away, her argumentative style was making Henry angrier than he had ever been in her presence. This wasn't a simple debate anymore - it had turned into a no holds barred confrontation. In other words, she was ruining everything.

"First of all, marrying for money is not a marriage - it's a business deal. A marriage of convenience is the same as going to a shoe store and picking the lower priced pair over the higher priced ones. *There's no emotion involved!*" he yelled. "If you only have $20 you buy the $20 shoes. You'll never know how the $40 ones feel because you're too lazy to wait a month to save up more money! As for arranged marriages - I think they're a huge waste of two productive lives! To me, a marriage should be entered into because you love your partner. And if they're financially and mentally stable - that's just extra icing on the cake!"

Tina stared at him in amazement. His face was beet red and perspiration had formed on his brow.

"Henry, get a grip!" After he took a couple of deep breaths she added, "How did we ever get on this subject anyway?"

"I asked about your feelings on marriage. That's all. Nothing else. I just wanted to know your feelings." Henry wiped his forehead with his shirtsleeve.

"And after all of this, did you get your answer?" Tina asked sheepishly.

"Well, you started off by calling it a pagan ritual entered into by two unsteady people. Then the Manson family was brought up, as was my financial stability. Then you took us back in time to relive a couple of your failed relationships, before getting into a discussion of ethics dealing with various marriage options."

"So aside from that pagan ritual quip I never really gave you an answer, right?"

"Don't worry about it. I'll give you another chance."

Henry stood up and reached into his pocket for the third time that night, pulling out the small blue box. Before Tina could comprehend what he was about to do, Henry knelt in front of her on one knee.

"So, I'll ask you again. What are your feelings about marriage?"

As she looked into Henry's hopeful eyes, the argument they had been having for the past twenty minutes quickly vanished.

"I think I'm going to love it, as much as I love you."

Henry took Tina's left hand and placed the engagement ring on her finger. As tears began to roll down her face, they were both startled by the sudden noises emitting from the television, as shock-host Spangler finally opened Jim Haggarty's locker.

"Oh my goodness! There must be a hundred Barbie dolls in here!" he screamed into the camera.

"I guess tonight was meant for surprises," Tina said hugging Henry.

"The difference being that, he'll go away in five minutes and I won't."

"Five minutes?" Tina reached for the remote and aimed it at the TV. "I was thinking more like five seconds!"

The two continued to kiss for several moments before Tina broke their embrace.

"Henry."

"Ah huh."

"What are your feelings about having six kids?"

"WHAT?"

"Forget it," she said beginning to kiss him again. "We'll discuss it later."

CHAPTER TWO

"Little Hopes & Dreams"

****

Doctor Theodore Ramsey walked down the corridor of the medical building holding a blue folder containing the test results of Tina Cole's physical. She, of course, was the picture of health and why shouldn't she be? Only twenty-five, she still had her whole life ahead of her. But the good doctor knew the news he was about to give her, could drastically change her plans for the future.

As the doctor closed the office door behind him, Tina immediately put down the magazine she was leafing through and smiled, anxiously awaiting his findings.

"Did I pass?" she asked.

"With flying colours," the doctor stated unequivocally, returning her grin. "But I did come across one very interesting finding."

"Oh, is that right?" Tina said nervously. "Anything to worry about?"

After thirty-five years as a general practitioner Dr. Ramsey had given literally hundreds of women the news he was about to bestow upon Tina Cole.

After hearing his medical conclusions some of his patients were ecstatic, while others wilted away before his eyes. Despite their facial or mental reaction, Dr. Ramsey was certain of one thing: they would all initially question his judgment - although few ever sought a second opinion.

"Are you sure?" Tina exclaimed after hearing she was pregnant. Dr. Ramsey smiled at her question. The chain remained unbroken, he thought.

"Yes I'm sure. I'm so sure, I'm positive," he quipped, seeing Tina had taken the news joyfully.

"I can't believe this. It seems like just yesterday Henry and I got married."

"It has been five years," the doctor reminded her as she got out of her chair. "You were always planning on having children weren't you?"

"Someday - but not now!" she replied. Her voice conveyed both anxiety and excitement. "Henry's gonna flip."

"That I'd like to see," the doctor laughed. "Now, what about your mother? What will she think of this blessed event?"

"My mother?" Tina said dreadfully. "She'll want to do everything!"

"Oh it can't be that bad. Anyway, that's what mothers are for, right?"

"You don't know my mother - yet," Tina said gleefully. "But I'm sure in the months ahead she'll make her presence felt - giving you some helpful advice on how best to care for her one and only daughter."

"I look forward to meeting her . . . I think,"

he said with a wink.

Tina walked over to Dr. Ramsey and gave him a hug. "Thank you for the wonderful news. I'm going to tell Henry as soon as he comes home."

Tina broke off the embrace and started toward the door. "I hope he's as happy about this as you are, Tina," the doctor said.

"I'm sure he will be," Tina responded exiting into the brightly lit outer office. "And if he isn't . . . he will be when I get through with him!"

As Tina disappeared around the corner, Dr. Ramsey closed the office door. Pushing his intercom button, he asked if his two o'clock appointment had arrived yet. Informed she hadn't, he thanked his secretary and pulled open the top drawer of his desk. Within it lay a cigar box that he opened only on special occasions.

"To Henry, Tina and their little one," he said gesturing a toast to his own children, whose photos hung on the far wall. "May all three of them find love and happiness together." With that part of his ritual over, he promptly bit off the tip of the cigar, reclined in his chair and savoured the taste of the chocolate as it slowly began to melt in his mouth.

****

Just as the doctor had predicted Tina's response to the pregnancy, he also knew what her husband's reaction would be. Although he lacked statistics to back him up, Dr. Ramsey was certain the shock would be short and hopefully sweet. Henry wouldn't disappoint him.

"You're what?"

"I'm pregnant. I mean we're pregnant! Do you know what this means, Henry?"

"You're going to spend all my money on a new wardrobe?"

"Aside from that," Tina said still excited.

"You're going to get very large?"

"Yeah, but besides that?"

"You're going to start to waddle instead of walk?"

"You're spoiling all the fun of this moment Henry Cole and I hate you for it!"

"I was kidding," he smiled as he gave Tina a congratulatory hug and kiss. "And I'll tell our boy that just as soon as he arrives."

"Boy? Who said anything about a boy, Mister?"

"Well I just assumed that with you being pregnant and all, you were going to bear us a son."

"Don't be too sure of yourself, Henry," Tina said pointing a finger at him. "If I had a boy my mother would never talk to me again!"

"See," Henry said triumphantly. "There's a great reason right there for having one."

"I'm going to tell her you said that," Tina retorted. "Then you'll really be in trouble."

They stood staring at each other in the hallway for a moment, the implications of this news hitting them simultaneously.

"Are you happy?" Tina asked in a quiet whisper.

"You know I am, babe." Tears appeared to well up in their eyes. "And you know what else I'm sure of?"

"No, what?"

"That I love you."

"I love you too, Henry."

Henry stepped forward and picked Tina off her feet, carrying and swinging her into the living room. "I'm going to be a Dad!" he proclaimed. "I'm going to be a Dad!"

The Coles' first decision as new parents-to-be was how to celebrate: go out on the town for dinner or opt to stay at home.

"I think we should celebrate in style," Henry proposed as he eagerly flipped through the telephone yellow pages. "What do you think - Shardini's or Lancio's?"

Tina was still in the living room looking up at their enlarged wedding picture. "How about Wacko's?" she said in a mischievous tone.

"Wacko's? Why on earth would you want to go to . . ."

"Because we've always gone there to commemorate a special event," Tina broke in. "I don't know why exactly - but we always have."

Henry pondered Tina's suggestion. It was true - no matter what the occasion they were always drawn back to the old place. "I really wasn't in the mood for a big juicy steak and champagne anyway," Henry laughed closing the phone book. "Wacko's it is!"

****

It had been about a year since their last visit, but as they approached the small building perched on a hill, it seemed like yesterday.

"It doesn't look like it's changed a bit, Henry," Tina said walking slowly to the front door.

"I think that's the whole purpose of this place."

Walking into Wacko's was like stepping back in time. Pictures of Elvis, James Dean and Marilyn adorned the walls, as did photos of Benny Goodman, Glenn Miller and The Beatles. Old album covers and 45's were thumb-tacked to the far wall, just over the vintage 1950's jukebox. Another wall was covered entirely in patron's old business cards. (A newspaper reporter recently ran an article on this 'wall of fame' and determined that of the 1046 companies represented, only 15 were still actively accepting customers.) The centerpiece of Wacko's was the long food counter. On one side of it was a row of chrome stools that were bolted to the black and white tiled floor. The red leather covered seats swiveled, making them perfect for talking to your friend on your right and then to the one on your left. On the other side of the counter were several old long-handled soda pop dispensers and a row of green milkshake blenders. The cash register was an antique, (probably worth more than the entire food inventory), but was used as casually as could be by the teenagers who kept

Wacko's youthful look intact. In short, it was a nostalgic dream come true.

"What would you like tonight?" the smiling waitress asked Henry as he and Tina approached the counter.

Henry would have loved to say, *The usual*, but he knew that would sound too hokey. "I think we'll have . . ." His voice trailed off as his eyes were again drawn to the row of paper plates (which constituted Wacko's menu) that hung just above the bright-eyed girl. "How about one Pizza Dog, one Hot As Heck Dog and an order of Chili Fries." Henry glanced over to Tina, who looked radiant even in blue jeans and a T-shirt, and smiled at her before turning back to the waitress. "And a strawberry shake," he said.

"Just one?" the waitress inquired.

"Just one," Henry said, his attention on Tina's smiling face again. "But with two straws please."

The girl said it would be a few minutes for their order, which she'd bring to their table when ready. After paying the tab, Henry led Tina down the row of booths that lined the wall opposite the counter.

"Was it this one," Henry pondered aloud, "or this one?"

"You tell me."

"Ah yes," Henry said proudly. "Here it is - our booth."

There was no mistaking it really. On the wooden seat - there for the whole world to see - was carved H.C. LOVES T.G.

Henry looked at the inscription. "It was true

six years ago when I met you and it's even truer today." He kissed Tina on the cheek and then shook his head. "And to think I was nineteen when I did that."

"If only you had had a pocket knife that night," Tina laughed as she sat down. "I don't think the owner was very impressed when you ruined two of his best stainless steel forks!"

"The spoon wasn't working too well if I remember correctly," Henry quipped.

In silence, they glanced around the restaurant. During the summertime, it was usually packed with teenagers who thought of it as their personal hangout, just as their parents had before them. Although it was a legendary landmark, Henry hadn't actually stepped into it until that first date with Tina. They were looking for somewhere different, somewhere abuzz with action. In other words: somewhere cheap.

"Do you think there will be a Wacko's when our *daughter* is a teenager?" Tina asked excitedly.

"Who knows - maybe our *son* will own the joint. The head wacko as it were!"

"Maybe you can give him some pointers."

"Are you saying I'm wacko?" Henry's face conveyed a look of hurt. "After all I've done for you."

"Don't you mean *to me*?" Tina chuckled patting her still flat stomach.

"Hey, hey, hey!" Henry protested. "It takes two to tango!"

"If we had kept to dancing, at least I would have been on my feet all the time," Tina retorted with a wink.

"Here's your order," the waitress said interrupting them. She placed the foot long hot dogs in front of them, along with their fries and strawberry milkshake.

Noticing there was only one straw in the large glass Henry asked, "Could we have another straw for the shake please?"

"Really?" she asked with a puzzled look on her face. "I thought you were joking." She ran around the counter, grabbed a second straw and dutifully plopped it into the thick drink. "How old are you two?" she asked outright.

"Twenty-five," Tina replied. "Is there a problem?"

"No. It's just that I've never seen two people your age act like this before. It's kinda scary." With that said she left them to enjoy their meal.

"Your age?" Henry laughed. "I wonder what she would have said if we'd told her you were expecting a child."

"She'd probably have called me Grandma or something!"

Henry cautiously bit into his Hot As Heck Dog, while Tina savoured the taste of her Pizza Dog.

"Do you feel old?" Tina asked timidly, almost blushing.

"We're twenty-five. When was that old?" Henry replied.

"When we were sixteen."

"You're not thinking about what Wendy the

Waitress said, are you?" Henry took a long sip of the shake in an attempt to cool his hot as heck taste buds.

"I just can't believe we have been married for five years already. And now this." Henry couldn't tell if Tina was just pulling his leg for the sake of argument or if she was serious. "Do you realize that when our daughter is twenty we'll be in our mid-forties?" Tina continued. "When she's our age we'll be fifty. Fifty years old, Henry!"

"I see your point, Tina," Henry said trying to sound sympathetic. "But where is it going? When we're a hundred and she's - I mean he's seventy-five?"

"I don't know," Tina said discouraged. "I just want to be certain that we're doing the right thing. Not that I don't want this baby - because I do - but that we'll be able to handle the added responsibility."

"We've handled other big responsibilities pretty well," Henry said taking a french fry smothered in chili into his mouth. "We got married without a hitch - and we're still happy together." He waited for her confirmation. "Right?"

"Of course we're still happy."

"And what about the house? We've managed to keep that bungalow from the bank for the past three years, correct? You've got a great career. I've got a great career. And you know what's best of all?" Tina glanced up at him with an expectant look. "Best of all," Henry started, taking Tina's hand in his, "we've got our whole lives in front of us. It doesn't matter if we're blessed with one child or ten children."

"Ten?" Tina asked skeptically.

"Maybe I was exaggerating a bit there. Nine will be fine." Tina laughed at the thought as Henry carried on. "But the point is that we have the opportunity to bring a new life into this world and that is the greatest gift we could ever give or be able to receive."

Up until this moment, Tina hadn't known just how excited or terrified Henry was of having a child. Now she knew she wouldn't have to go through the next several months alone. Their marriage truly was a partnership. Henry's eyes seemed to glass over for a moment, as did Tina's.

"We're going to love this child with everything we've got," Henry said leaning over the milkshake. Tina leaned forward meeting him halfway.

As they gently kissed one another, they were unaware their young waitress was watching them. "I bet they're newlyweds," she said, clutching her notepad to her heart. "Isn't love grand?"

Henry looked toward the jukebox.

"Do you think they've stocked 'You're Having My Baby' in that old thing?"

"Let's hope not," Tina groaned watching Henry walk over to the machine, digging in his pocket for change. As the record Henry had selected dropped into place, he rejoined Tina in the booth, this time sitting close beside her. "You didn't pick anything really corny did you?"

"Let's just say I chose an appropriate selection to honour today's auspicious occasion. And as I feel like a King myself tonight, I thought, who better to help celebrate with than another King."

The initial crackle of the old 45 made the other patrons in Wacko's take notice. As the song proceeded along, it appeared as if everyone in attendance - both young and old (meaning those twenty-five or older) - knew the words.

"You don't think Elvis Presley singing 'Teddy Bear' isn't just a bit corny?"

"Not at all," Henry said wrapping his arm around Tina. "Do you?"

Snuggling up to his shoulder Tina just smiled. "Nope. Not at all."

Like Elvis, Henry and Tina also had to finally leave the building. They headed toward the lakefront, with tall ice cream cones in hand.

"In a few months, we won't be able to come here anymore for ice cream," Henry said.

"Why is that?"

"Because I didn't see a chocolate-pickle-peanut butter flavour there. Or even an olive-strawberry-bratwurst mixture. What's a poor pregnant woman to do?"

"Buy a blender and create new flavours at home?"

"It's probably cheaper by the pint that way."

Crossing the wooden bridge to the beach Tina stopped and peered at their reflections in the calm stream below them. "Do you think we'll be good parents, Henry? I mean I know we'll be great parents, but do you think in the end - even with all our good intentions - that we'll end up acting just like our parents did?"

"I think every couple faced with a child in their future swears things will be done differently than when they were growing up. That they'll let their children be more independent than they were ever allowed to be. That they won't become their parents come hell or high water."

"Are you one of those radicals, Henry - ready to banish the old ways for the new?"

"I don't think so," he said contemplating his own childhood. "I liked my parents. A little strict now and then mind you, but that goes with the territory. It's inherent. I think all those radicals who swear up and down, usually come from pretty poor family backgrounds in the first place. They just grow up and grow older getting more and more angry with themselves." He turned to face Tina. "Luckily we didn't come from that kind of a background, so we're left to our own devises and judgments. If we screw up now and then, we'll simply chalk it up to experience."

"Or lack of it," Tina cut in nervously. "There's just so much to learn - to understand. I'm an only child. What do I know about raising kids? You had Barb to take care of. You have some experience. What experience do I have with children?" She looked up from the water and saw that Henry was on the verge of laughing aloud.

"You've been married to me for five years, right? What else do you need to know about childish behaviour?" Henry gazed down the path of the stream that stretched out in front of them. "Of course you didn't have to potty train me," he chuckled.

"Potty training?" The worried, confused look unexpectedly reappeared on Tina's face.

"Hey, babe, just chill out. That's not for a couple of years yet!" Again Henry laughed.

"You sound pretty sure of yourself, Mr. Cole. You wouldn't by any chance have children bearing your likeness scattered across the countryside would you?"

"None that I know of," he deadpanned.

"There had better not be," Tina said sternly, as a wide smile washed over her troubled features. Suddenly she ran off the bridge and headed onto the sandy beach, kicking her shoes off as she went. "Tonight we're not going to worry about the future!" she yelled back to Henry. "Tonight we celebrate!"

Henry quickly finished off his ice cream and joined Tina, who was now waist high in warm lake water.

"Do you want to skinny dip, Henry?" she asked devilishly, starting to unbutton his shirt.

"Here?" he said in protest. "Right now?"

"Why not?"

"What if somebody walks by and sees us?" Henry asked looking nervously up and down the beach.

"We'll just tell them we're celebrating the conception of our first child!" Tina managed to lift Henry's shirt off his back and started on his belt buckle.

"You certainly are full of energy tonight," he said starting to enjoy the scenario being laid out in front of him.

"It must be my hormones," Tina said deliriously. "They're probably working overtime with the baby and all!"

Soon they were splashing and laughing together amid the soothing lull of the waves. It would be one night they swore never to forget. It would also be the beginning of the most painful period in their lives as a married couple.

****

With just eight weeks left before her due date, Tina began to feel pains in her stomach. It had nothing to do with the baby's frisky kicking from within. It was a pain that would not go away.

Henry was immediately informed at the office that Tina was about to go into emergency surgery. As he raced to the hospital, his only thoughts were of the baby and of course his wife. To this point it had been an easy pregnancy - the doctor telling them everything was fine and the baby appeared to be healthy. Henry was always wary of any phrase that had the word *appeared* in it, instead of *was* or *wasn't*." As he ran into the emergency ward he knew that everything in fact *wasn't* right - no matter how it *appeared*.

As a crescent moon began to rise high in the night sky outside of her hospital room window, Tina awoke feeling groggy. The sedatives she'd been given were still having a strong effect on her. In the corner of the room, she could see Henry slouched in a chair, sleeping in his rumpled business suit - his jacket acting as a blanket. Now, even before she looked at her mid-section, she knew the dream was over. Staring at the white sterile sheet resting flat on her stomach, confirmed only too well, her worst fears.

As the tears and anguish began to pour from deep within her, she cried out Henry's name, waking him instantly.

"The baby," Tina sobbed. "Our baby."

Wordlessly Henry went to the side of the bed and leaned over to embrace his wife.

"They took our baby."

Henry continued to hold Tina, feeling helpless as her body convulsed with suffering - both mental and physical.

"It's okay, Tina," he whispered, trying to soothe her. He pulled away slightly and kissed her trembling lips, tasting her salty tears. "You're alive. That's what's important."

"How can you say that?" Tina asked, shocked by what she thought was her husband's callous appraisal of the situation. "It was a little baby, Henry. Our baby." Again the emotion was too much and she deteriorated into tears and sobs of overwhelming heartache.

Dr. Ramsey and two nurses were soon in the room and asked Henry to step aside for a moment as they checked Tina's vital signs. Standing in the corner, Henry could see the effect this event was having on his grieving wife. Her cheeks were now stained from crying and her hair was wet with perspiration. She seemed to pay no attention to the medical staff working around her, but simply looked toward the window, her face gaunt and pale.

Henry knew one facet of this case that Tina hadn't been told of yet. After witnessing her reaction to the sudden realization that she'd lost their first child, he was unsure how she'd take the news she would be unable to bear any children in the years to come. Once the nurses had left, Dr. Ramsey told her the diagnosis. For a moment, Henry was frightened as he saw all the life drain from Tina's face.

In the weeks following her release from the hospital, much to Henry's relief Tina slowly pulled out of her depression and started to return to her old self again - albeit a little more reserved than before. They had talked at length of their future together. One thing had become perfectly clear: children or no children, they could always depend on each other.

"What about a dog?"

"Excuse me?" Henry couldn't believe his ears. They were sitting in the living room reading with the TV volume down low, when Tina had brought forth her startling suggestion.

"A dog," Tina reiterated. "You know - four legs and a tail. Barks at strangers. Humps the legs of friends and family."

"Yeah, I know what a dog is, Tina," Henry said, still suspicious of the proposal. "Are you sure you really want a dog? You know - so soon after the . . ."

"You can say it, Henry. So soon after the miscarriage and the news."

"I just don't want you to rush into anything

that would . . . I don't know . . ."

"Set me back?"

"Yes, I guess that's what I mean."

"Well, let me tell you something, Mister Cole," Tina started. Just from the tone of her voice, Henry knew she was on the verge of making her successful return. "As a man, you know nothing about giving birth or carrying a child. Carrying a mortgage maybe - but it's not the same thing. Would you agree?" Astonished by her candour and the playfulness in her voice, Henry quickly concurred. "So you know nothing about the bonding process that goes on between a child and its mother, right?" She didn't wait for an answer. "To put it into layman's terms for you - it's awesome. And lately I've begun to miss that feeling. You know the one: wanting to hold something in your arms, knowing it's yours, knowing that it loves you as much as you love it. It makes you feel alive."

Henry could see that Tina's eyes were beginning to water over, but she insisted on continuing her reasons for wanting a dog. At the first sign of tears rolling down her cheek, Henry wanted to go to her and hold her, all the while telling her she wasn't at fault for what happened, and that he'd always love her. As she continued however, he realized this was something she had to do - for herself, and for them. It was part of the healing process. After weeks of fighting it, she'd decided now was the time to embrace it.

"It wouldn't even have to be a puppy. Maybe we could get an older dog or something. That way you don't have to paper train them or get up in the middle of the night hearing them whining for affection. I think a middle-aged dog would be good, don't you?" Again she didn't wait for Henry's reply. "With a dog like that, you don't have to worry about them so much - if they're going to rip apart the couch or make a travesty out of the garden. Best of all they'd love you for who you are and not for how much time you played with them as a pup, rolling like an idiot on the floor." Tina tried to choke back her tears. "So how about it, Henry? Do you want to get a dog or what?"

The question was rhetorical. Henry finally walked over to Tina and held her tight. Both cried on the other's shoulder.

"I'd love a dog, Tina," he said gently. "And I love you."

"I love you too, Henry. I really do." Tina held onto him as if fearing that once he had broken off her hold, he'd never return for another hug. "And I'm sorry about the baby."

"You have nothing to be sorry about," Henry said. "Who knows - maybe this was a sign of some sort."

"Do you really think so?" Tina asked loosening her grip slightly.

"Maybe we were never cut out to be parents." Henry knelt beside Tina's chair and looked into her puffy red eyes. "Maybe we would have turned out to be like the parents of kids we hated in school." Tina laughed at Henry's attempt to humour her; to help pull her back from the edge. "Maybe we'd turn out to be like the parents of a girl I used to date."

"Oh yeah," Tina said suspiciously, wiping another tear away. "Go on."

"Well this girl's parents were so strict . . ." Henry waited for Tina to play his straight man, as she had so willingly done in the past.

"How strict were they?" she asked, a smile awaiting the punch line.

"They were so strict that the only way I could take their daughter to the drive-in was if we went to the matinee show."

Tina stared back at him puzzled. "I don't get it."

"Matinee . . . The drive-in . . ." Henry said trying to coax her along.

"Yeah, so?"

"Matinees are shown in the afternoon." Still no uproarious laughter. "At the drive-in it has to be dark . . ."

A look of comprehension finally crossed Tina's face. "Oh I get it now." She paused a moment. "What a stupid joke. One of your own, right?"

"Straight from my little brain to yours," Henry said kissing her forehead.

"Should I be offended by that comment?"

"You can be whatever you want."

"Great!" Tina said raising one hand in the air, while brushing aside the final tears from her cheek. "I want to be a dog owner then."

"Your wish is my command."

Standing up they looked into each other's swollen, tear stained faces.

"Tina, I hope you know that no matter what happens during our marriage, I will always stand by you," Henry said tenderly.

"I never doubted that for a minute, Henry." She pushed up on her tip toes and kissed him. "You know - there are certain advantages of not being able to get pregnant again," Tina continued with a devilish grin.

"No dirty diapers to change?" Henry joked.

"You're not even warm."

"We can soon fix that."

Henry lifted Tina in his arms and started up the stairs to their bedroom.

"I've heard some of the guys at work complaining their kids sometimes come into the bedroom at very inappropriate times," Henry said lying beside Tina on their queen-sized bed.

"Did they say anything about their dogs?"

"Nothing."

"Advantage number one!" Tina said beginning to kiss Henry's neck.

"Are you sure you don't want a cat instead?"

"Now why would I want two hairy animals in this house who just sit around all day watching TV?"

"Should I take offence to that remark?"

Tina planted a wet kiss on Henry's lips. "My advice to you," she said smiling, "is to take it anyway you want."

****

From that afternoon on, both realized the future was theirs for the taking. They had only each other now. Luckily, that was all they would ever need.

CHAPTER THREE

"Paging, Dr. Stevens"

****

*T*he air in the kitchen was cool as a morning breeze came through the open window above the sink. It was the first truly nice day of spring and had arrived just in time for Tina's liking. As she cracked a couple of eggs on the side of the skillet, she heard Henry walk into the room.

"Excuse me, Miss - have you seen my wife?"

"Not since she was making out with the milk man this morning," Tina said innocently as she threw the egg shells into the nearby garbage can.

"That's really discouraging," Henry said, sitting down at the kitchen table.

"And why is that, sir?"

"Because we owe the paperboy so much!"

"You are a pig!" Tina exclaimed. Turning suddenly, she threw the spatula in Henry's general direction. With split second timing, he was able to deflect it with his newspaper, sending it harmlessly to the floor.

"As a former farm girl, I guess you've known

quite a few of us."

"But you're the only one I've ever slept with," Tina countered, bending over to give Henry a morning kiss.

"Ah, lucky me, to be cast so perfectly in your little life-play, The Pig and I."

Tina just smiled as Henry began to laugh.

"Do you know why I married you?"

"Not off hand. Why do you ask?"

"Because my mother keeps wanting to know, and for the life of me I can never give her a good enough reason."

"Ha, ha, ha."

Henry quickly immersed himself in the financial section as Tina continued to prepare his breakfast.

"How would you like your eggs - fried, fried or fried?" she asked.

"I usually like scrambled," Henry began, not missing a line of newsprint. "But what does the chef recommend?"

"Fried is always good."

"Then fried it is!" he exclaimed. "Isn't it wonderful, honey, to live in a country where you have the freedom to choose whatever your wife wants?"

"It's in the Constitution, isn't it?" Tina asked with a smile.

Henry put his paper aside as Tina let the eggs slide onto his plate. As per usual, they looked great.

"Aren't you going to have any?" Henry questioned, seeing Tina put the skillet in the sink.

"Are you kidding? Those things'll kill you!"

she announced.

Henry gingerly took a bite of one of his eggs. "Do you mean eggs in general or these two eggs specifically?"

"What's the difference?"

"Well . . . if you're talking in general terms - fine. But if you've poisoned these two eggs specifically, I think I have the right to know."

"Why? Are you afraid of death, Big Boy?"

"Death, no." Henry flipped the remainder of the eggs over with his fork and examined them more closely. "It's just I have my big presentation to make today and I'd hate to drop dead during it, causing me to really embarrass myself."

"Don't worry about making a fool of yourself. The presentation will go fine."

"I hope so."

"I'm sure there's someone else at your office who can make it for you. Posthumously, of course."

Henry ate the final piece of egg and stood up, kissing Tina again before putting his dish in the sink.

"You're a real firecracker this morning, aren't you?" Henry grabbed the coffee pot and poured himself a cup. "I have to sell the firm to the largest account to ever walk through our doors and you're telling me now I could die prematurely. I don't know which one is worse."

Henry noticed that Tina's attention was no longer focused on him, but on a page in the Lifestyle section of his newspaper. He wasn't surprised, as everyday she did the same thing: skip over the major headlines and go straight to her horoscope and astrochart.

"So what have those crackpots written today?" he joked.

"Well, it says here that a financial bonanza is yours for the asking. Colleagues will reward you generously for a job well done. And a dark, romantic stranger will heighten your love life."

"With all that going for me - I can't go wrong!" Henry said ecstatically.

"What?" Tina peered over the top of the paper with a puzzled look on her face. "You're not a Gemini! That was *my* horoscope! Now you're an Aries . . ." Tina glanced down at the paper again. "It says beware of food connected with chickens. Delegate office workload to others. Your health is of utmost concern today. And finally . . ."

"There's more good news?"

"And finally - that pain in your chest could be much worse than simple heartburn."

"Are you sure you've read everything?"

Tina pulled the paper close to her face. "Hold on. In small print it says you should check all insurance policies before 10 a.m." Tina put the section back on the table in a crumpled pile. "Oh - and have a nice day," she added with a smirk.

"You know, dear, I can't figure out why we spend so much money on defense in this country. For a small fee you could just phone up the superpowers every morning and read them their horoscopes!"

"Do you really think it would work?" Tina asked with a glint in her eye.

Henry returned her stare as they yelled in unison, "Naaa!"

"I'd better get going," Henry said, walking toward the back door, picking up the briefcase that sat waiting for him there. "Aren't you going to wish me good luck?"

"Break a leg!"

"That sounds more like an order than a wish of luck."

"You know, I was just thinking, Henry, maybe you'd get lucky and break your leg," Tina said, walking up to him. "That way during the presentation you'd be guaranteed the sympathy vote."

"I never thought of it that way. Thanks . . . I think."

As Henry closed the door behind him, Tina yelled, "Good luck!" before heading back to the table. There she again picked up the paper and began to reread her horoscope.

"A dark stranger. Heightened love life. Money! This could be my lucky day!"

****

Henry had never been so nervous in his life. Although he was one of the top salesmen at Markinson & Leonard's Advertising, he could never overcome pre-presentation jitters - no matter how important or insignificant the client was.

The first time he had ever stood in front of his peers, he wet his pants. Luckily, he was only six years old at the time. It was during his first stint as Show and Tell Master of Ceremonies that his 'accident' occurred. It was bad enough that he only had his teddy bear to show off (the one that helped him escape enemies from the planet Zublic each night), without being so frightened as to lose control of his bodily functions. Even today, the memory haunted him.

He had rehearsed his pitch repeatedly, but somehow the words just didn't quite gel together as well as he'd hoped. Driving to his downtown office, he gave it another go around.

"So as you can see gentlemen, Ritzer's products could not only save you lots and lots of money . . . No, not lots and lots. What word am I looking for? Could not only save you huge? Huge amounts of money. . . No, I sound like a used car dealer. Then what? Could save you an enormous amount of money . . . Now that's not too bad, but these guys are from a foreign country - probably don't speak much English. So – what if I use some slang words on them? Like what . . . How about, Ritzer's products could not only save you gobs of money . . . No, that sounds too vulgar . . . What about *whole lots*?. . . Ritzer's products could not only save you whole lots of money, they could also . . ."

Henry let this train of thought die as he was beginning to get discouraged about how he was going to pull off this presentation.

"I'm dead. Up the creek. A drowning man in a pit of quicksand," he said, throwing up his hands. "I have to calm down. *Calm down, Henry*," he told his rearview mirror twin. "It'll be okay. What you need right now is to take a deep breath," - he inhaled deeply - "and take lots of pills for this headache. Where are those things?"

Seeing that the traffic in front of him was still pretty light, Henry reached over and fumbled through the glove box. "Ah ha!" he cried, as his fingers located a small pill bottle. Opening it he palmed four white pills, popped them into his mouth, and washed them down with the coffee in his mug, which was resting precariously on top of the dash.

"Just have to relax old boy. Everything'll be fine."

Henry settled himself back into his seat and threw the bottle on the empty seat beside him.

"Nothing's going to go wrong today," he said confidently.

****

Ellen Faber had been Tina's best friend since she'd moved in next door four years earlier. Ellen's marriage was on the rocks and within a year Samuel Faber had vacated the property. Now a full-time divorcee, Ellen popped by as often as possible - much to Henry's displeasure and Tina's delight.

On first examination, aside from being the same age – forty-two - Ellen and Tina had very little in common. Ellen was, for all intents and purposes, still a child of the sixties. Her rustic strawberry blonde hair was always braided in impossible designs and her clothes looked like they were her '60's originals'. However, Tina knew for a fact that Ellen actually bought the psychedelic wear new from a shop in New York. Every year Ellen would trek to the Big Apple with the sole intention of buying these trendy new, old clothes. The Grateful Dead was her favourite group, of course.

Tina, on the other hand, was much more cosmopolitan. She never considered herself to be on the cutting edge of fashion, but she did pride herself on at least keeping abreast of the current trends. Her short bobbed hairstyle for instance, was all the rage now, even though she had worn it this way for the past seven years. "What goes around comes around," she was fond of saying. As for her favourite recording artists? Old Chicago and Bruce Springsteen (before Born In The U.S.A.) albums came readily to mind.

"I can't believe Jane told Larry to get out!"

"It was bound to happen, Ellen."

Tina returned to the living room and poured Ellen another cup of international coffee. ("That regular stuff will kill ya!" Ellen often protested. "Do you know what they put in there?") Ellen took a sip of the steamy liquid and then continued their conversation. "What would you have done if Henry had acted like Larry?"

"What would I have done?" Tina placed the coffee pot on a ceramic coaster on the table and sat opposite Ellen. "Well . . . after I'd found out he was a transvestite Go-Go dancer at the roadhouse, I think I would rethink my marriage vows, number one. And, if I were told by my teenage son's girlfriend, that my beloved Henry was really her father - due to some sort of miscalculation sixteen years earlier -

I would definitely consult with my minister, number two. And if after all that, Henry cancelled plans with me so he could go out with the boys for some 'fun and games', I'd probably do the same thing as Jane - throw him out!"

Ellen pondered Tina's response. "I never thought of it that way. But after you threw him out, would you still love him?"

"Who - Henry or Larry?"

"Henry."

"Of course I'd still love him, don't be stupid. I'd always love that big goof."

"I just hope that Jane feels the same toward Larry."

"It is just a television show, Ellen! By next season, Jane will be back in the convent. And do you know what?"

"What?" Ellen asked anxiously.

"By the third week, she'll have broken at least - *at least* - four commandments!"

"How can you know for sure?"

"I can't reveal my sources mind you, but it's 95% certain to happen."

"You don't say." Ellen lifted her cup to her lips and soberly sipped her coffee. Tina tried everything in her power not to laugh aloud.

"If people could get as involved in politics in this country as you do over a stupid soap, Ellen, the rest of the world would be putty in our hands."

"Don't you ever get excited?" Ellen asked defensively.

"Not over a TV program."

"What about Henry? As an ad exec, he must get excited about things - you know, the campaigns or commercials or magazine ads."

"He gets excited all right," Tina said, beginning to smile. "When he left here today, he was probably too excited for his own good."

****

The morning traffic had not yet substantially increased in volume, which was just fine with Henry, who was still going over his impending presentation. Nothing seemed to be going right. How would the graphics work? Would they understand what he was saying? Again, did they even speak English? A thousand other questions flew through his mind. Fortunately the pills had started to do their work. Henry was more physically relaxed than he had been for days - even weeks. The tension in his shoulders and back seemed to have just melted away. So while his mind was in a furious competition with Mr. Wizard for the answers to his numerous questions, his muscles slowly began to feel like gelatin.

"Boy, do these things work fast," Henry said turning the corner.

The day was hot, but not hot enough to make him perspire as profusely as he was now. As a bead of sweat dripped over his eyebrow and into his eye, Henry sluggishly raised his hand to clear his vision. His eyesight was impaired for just a few seconds, but that was more than enough time for calamity to strike. As his vision adjusted itself back to the bright daylight, the last thing Henry saw was a street vendor's hot dog cart explode as his car rammed through it. A shower of freshly cooked wieners, sausages and buns cascaded over the front windshield. The car and cart finally came to an abrupt stop as Henry slammed on the brakes.

Unfortunately, Henry was no longer conscious to witness the mayhem that now surrounded him.

****

After Ellen had left, Tina decided to relax a bit and start reading the mystery novel she had put off for the past few weeks. She had barely gotten started when the phone rang.

'Hello . . . Yes, this is Tina Cole. An accident? Is he okay?" Tina's voice began to quiver at the thought of Henry in some emergency ward all alone. "Where did they take him? St. Peter's? No, it's okay. I can get there myself. Thank you for calling."

Tina slowly replaced the receiver and slumped onto the couch, sending her book falling to the floor. After getting control of her thoughts, she quickly began to dial a number.

"Hello, Mom? Could you go to the hospital with me? Henry's been in a terrible accident."

Selma Gordon was at the house in no time and wasn't surprised to see Tina waiting for her out on the front step. Aside from a few words about what the police officer had said - and directions to the hospital - neither of them spoke. The ride was a short one. Once in the emergency ward, Tina acted like a cub reporter in search of a scoop, trying to get all the necessary information pertaining to Henry's condition in record time. Regrettably, none was forthcoming.

After being told a doctor would be by to update them shortly, Tina and her mother found themselves sitting in a greyish-green waiting room. Tina held her head in her hands, while Selma glanced at the assorted magazines on the table beside her.

"Dear, you have to get hold of yourself. If Henry's up and about you'll look foolish for worrying so much."

Tina lifted her head and glared at her mother. "But what if he's not all right, Mom? What then? And why didn't the police tell me how he was?"

Selma's face remained unemotional, as she continued to turn magazine pages. "Because they don't want to worry any family members. So, they just pass the responsibility on to the doctors to tell the loved ones about the patient's condition. The officer didn't tell you, because he didn't know," Selma stated flatly. "It's not his job to know. Or to tell."

"No guts, if you ask me!"

"You're taking this whole thing far too personally, Tina."

"*Too personally?*" Tina screamed, bolting from her chair. "How can you take the loss of a loved one too personally?"

"He's not lost, dear," Selma said calmly.

"Yet!"

Selma could see that Tina was trying her hardest not to start to cry, but the emotion was just

Call it off!

Times change.

"In our life, Tina, many things happen that we don't plan for - that we can't plan for. They just happen, and we have to deal with them the best way we know how." It was Selma's turn to reminisce of the past. "Now when your father died, I had very mixed feelings about it. Although we'd both agree that our love for each other dried up years before, we still had a strong relationship that spanned more than forty-five years. You can't just forget that overnight. Now as far as you and Henry are concerned, you love one another very much. And that's what counts. That's what will get you through the rough times. If you find out something unthinkable has happened, you two will work it out somehow." Selma paused before adding, "That's the power of love, my dear."

It was truly a miracle. "Thanks, Mom, I think I'm ready for any bad news now," Tina said, sitting up straight and wiping the tears from her eyes. "If he's crippled or paralyzed, I'll stay by his side. And if he has brain damage and can't think for himself - then I'll think for both of us. I'll just have to. I love him that much."

****

The air in Henry's room had the same sterile smell that occupied all the corridors and waiting rooms of St. Peter's Hospital. Like Tina, its effects had given Henry a headache and made his stomach queasy. Also contributing to his ill feeling were the painkillers he'd taken for his broken leg - which now hung in the air by ropes and pulleys.

"A simple fracture, Mr. Cole," Dr. Stevens said, filling in his chart. "You're lucky it wasn't worse."

"How's the hot dog vendor?" Henry asked sheepishly.

"Apparently he wasn't hurt, but his cart is a write-off."

"From what I remember, it went right off my hood," Henry laughed.

"You'll be glad to hear that the police officer said there would be no charges laid against you. The old guy admitted crossing against traffic."

"A good break for me, eh?" Henry laughed again, tapping his cast. "I wonder if he'll ever get another hot dog cart."

Putting the medical chart back on its peg, Dr. Stevens broke into a wide smile. "Oh, I'm sure he'll *relish* the day he *mustards* up enough money for a new cart. Then he can start to *ketchup* for lost business."

"Ooh, that was bad," Henry said holding his stomach as he laughed out loud. "Do all you doctors have this kind of bedside humour?"

"Unfortunately not. But most of my patients seem to enjoy it."

"Count me as one of them."

"I will. Now you get your rest and I'll keep an eye open for your wife," Dr. Stevens said, walking out into the hallway.

As the doctor disappeared from view, Henry

couldn't resist yelling some friendly advice to him. "You better keep both eyes open, Doc! She's quite a looker!"

****

It had been one of the most excruciating hours of Tina's life. With every second came dread. With every doctor walking down the hall came confirmation of her anxiety. So when Dr. Stevens finally appeared in the doorway, a sense of doom came with him.

"Mrs. Cole?"

"Yes, that's me. How's my husband?"

"Well, I have some good news and some bad news."

Selma slipped her hand into Tina's, squeezing it tightly. It was the moment of truth.

"I'm ready for the bad news," Tina said, her voice trembling slightly.

"The bad news is that he won't be able to walk."

"Oh my God," both Tina and her mother exclaimed as they hugged each other for support.

"But the good news is," the doctor continued, "that it'll only be for six or seven weeks."

From the look on Tina's face as she broke from her mother's embrace, he could tell something was wrong.

"What was that?" Tina asked slowly, wiping her tears away.

"Well . . . when he hit that hot dog vendor

downtown," Dr. Stevens stuttered, "he broke his right leg."

"We weren't told any of this, doctor," Selma declared.

"Was he hurt anywhere else?" Tina inquired with a tinge of bitterness in her voice.

"I'm terribly sorry," the good doctor said apologizing. "I just assumed you had already been told. Please excuse my somewhat warped sense of humour." He was greeted by faint traces of smiles on the faces of the two women before him. "But as for any other injuries, he probably hurt his pride a little." The doctor pulled a pill bottle from his smock. "You see, he accidentally took these pills to calm his nerves while driving. He had some kind of presentation today? Well . . . the pills weren't aspirins - they were muscle relaxants!"

"*What?*" Selma exclaimed.

"They were his sister Barb's when she went into labour last year," Tina said laughing hysterically.

With the tension now evaporated, Dr. Stevens also laughed. "Those would be the ones. They took effect quite rapidly and Henry was unable to stop his car in time. But no charges will be laid I'm told," he added.

Selma looked up at the doctor. "So that's where all those wieners came from on Winchester Street."

"If you want to see your husband," the doctor addressed Tina, "he's just down the corridor in room #408."

"Thank you very much, doctor," Tina said. "Six weeks you say?"

"At least."

As the doctor walked out of the waiting room, Selma started to get up from her chair.

"Ah . . . I want to speak to Henry alone for a few minutes, Mom. Do you mind?" Tina asked sweetly.

"No, not at all, dear," her mother replied with a knowing smile.

"I thought so."

Tina walked down the corridor until she located room #408. Entering it, she was surprised by how dark it was inside. She quickly realized that the weather had turned nasty since her arrival. The clouds had rolled in and it was almost pitch dark outside as rain hit the outer windows. The only real illumination in the room emitted from the patients' overhead bed lights. Tina looked at the four faces staring at her before zeroing in on Henry's bed. "Why aren't you dead?" she yelled.

"Look fellas - it's Tina, my loving wife that I've been telling you about!" Henry joked.

"Hi, Tina!" the other three men shouted before going back to the books and magazines they'd been reading.

"Hi, fellas," she replied. "Now you . . ." Tina said angrily, walking briskly to Henry's side. "I was worried to tears that something major had happened, you *wiener*!"

"Oh please, don't mention wieners - or relaxants!"

"Don't you ever read the labels on drug bottles?" Tina scolded him. "They're serious when they say, DO NOT operate heavy machinery after taking prescribed dosage."

"I always thought they meant like a stove or a bulldozer," Henry said blushing as Tina took his hand in hers.

"You had me *really* worried. I was thinking about all sorts of terrible situations."

"Were you ever going to leave me if one of those situations had happened?"

"Only if one particular area of your body was damaged beyond repair," Tina laughed.

"I hope it wasn't my right leg," Henry said, returning her smile.

"You're safe - it wasn't the *right* one."

"Thank goodness. You had me worried there for a minute."

"Don't give me that worried guff," Tina shot back, only half kidding. "I was the real one who was worrying while you lay here on your back all comfortable - pretty nurses doting on your every request."

"Well, not every request."

"I think you should know I got some real inspiration for sticking by you from a very unlikely source."

"The hot dog vendor?"

"No. My mother."

"Your mother? My mother-in-law?" Henry exclaimed.

"The one and only," Tina said triumphantly.

"And let's keep her the one and only. When she finds out what really happened, she's going to take back every kind word she said about me - and then she'll up and break my other leg!"

"No, she won't," Tina said with a wink.

"Really?"

"I made her promise."

"What a relief."

"Move over," Tina ordered as she hopped up on the bed. "I wonder how your presentation went today without you?"

"Well, I did break my leg, so we'll at least get their sympathy vote, right?" Henry asked, running Tina's hand over the cast. "And by the way, how did your horoscope predictions turn out?"

"Well . . . " Tina began with a sigh. "My financial situation is unchanged. And as I had the day off from work, my colleagues couldn't reward me for a job well done. So that just leaves . . ."

"A dark stranger," Henry said finishing her sentence.

"He didn't appear - but don't think I didn't give him some thought! I guess it wasn't meant to be," Tina said shrugging her shoulders. "Mother says some things just happen that we have no control over and we have to adjust to them. So I guess the same holds true for things that don't happen, right?"

"Yeah - maybe." From her mischievous tone, Henry knew Tina was up to something. Suddenly she jumped to the floor and started to close the curtains around the bed.

"What if the newspaper meant a strange

situation would heighten my love life?" she asked with a crafty smile. "Now what's stranger than the love of my life breaking his leg, after creaming a wiener cart?"

"I think I'm following you," Henry said, as Tina rejoined him on the bed. "So we now have the stranger part and the love life part, but where does the dark part come in?"

Tina leaned toward Henry to kiss him while also reaching for the overhead light cord.

"The dark part comes when I pull this little string," she said in a sexy whisper.

"Oh."

The other three male occupants of the room - who had been carefully monitoring their roommate's situation - silently decided to go for a walk to give the two lovebirds a little privacy. Closing the door behind them, they began their stroll down the corridor.

"With a nurse like that at home, Henry is going to be up and walking in no time," one of them said chuckling.

"Why would he want to do that?" asked another. All three were laughing at the implication when they were stopped by a woman in her early sixties.

"Do you know where room #408 is?" she asked. "I'm looking for my daughter and son-in-law."

"Ah . . ." was all they could say as they looked at one another. "I think they've just taken him back to x-ray, ma'am. We're his roomies, so to speak," the youngest of them stammered.

"Are you sure?" Selma asked in disbelief. "I thought they'd already set his leg."

"Well, yeah . . . they did, but on closer examination they thought the other leg may be broken also. You know how doctors are."

"Do you know how long he'll be? My soaps are coming on soon."

"I don't know," the spokesman of the group said. "At least an hour - right guys?"

"Yeah, at least."

"Maybe two, ma'am. You know how hospitals run."

Selma, who was not paying much attention to the three nervous gentlemen in front of her, located the door to Henry's room. "I think I'd better check just in case."

"No!" the three yelled simultaneously.

"Ah, what we meant was, there is no need to check - we just came from there. Henry's gone and so is his wife . . . Tina, right?"

"Yes, that's my daughter."

"They just left. Honest."

Selma still had a glum expression on her face. "What about my soaps?"

"Soaps?" the tallest patient spoke up, putting his arm around Selma's broad shoulders. "If you come with us we'll lead you right to a waiting room that has a nice colour TV. Does that sound all right? That way you can enjoy your shows while the others . . . ah, enjoy themselves."

"How can you enjoy yourself with a broken leg?" Selma asked skeptically.

"I meant enjoy each other's company - right guys?"

"Yeah, that's right."

"I've never enjoyed Henry's company," Selma began, taking one last glance toward room #408 before being whisked down the hall by her three new friends. "Do you know he once put a whoopee cushion under my seat?"

"No!"

"Oh yes he did!"

Back in the room Tina stopped kissing Henry for a moment and turned her ear toward the door.

"Did you hear my mother just then?"

"Now why would I do that?"

"She is roaming this hospital you know."

"But she wouldn't dare pull back the curtains around a hospital bed that just happened to be in total darkness, *would she*?"

"I guess you're right."

"I know I'm right. So stop acting like a frightened teenager in your parents' house."

"And what did you have in mind, Henry?"

Henry gently pulled Tina's face to his and kissed her lightly.

"That's Dr. Cole to you."

"I like the sound of that."

"And I think I'm going to like being laid up in a bed for the next few weeks."

"Oh would you shut up already!"

While Tina and Henry were playing "Doctor" just down the hall Selma enjoyed her daily prescription of love in the afternoon. As for Henry's accommodating roommates - they endured Selma, her beloved soaps and her horror stories of Henry until Tina finally came to their rescue. Walking into the waiting room, she once again greeted them with a very wide smile on her face.

<u>*CHAPTER FOUR*</u>

"The High Roller Blues"

****

*I*n the thirteen intervening years since Henry's automobile "mishap", the Coles' lives had changed, but not drastically. With only a few years to go before they could both take an early retirement - Henry from the advertising business and Tina from the interior design industry - they had to admit their marriage was as strong as ever. Although, they still didn't see eye to eye on everything.

"They did what?" Henry exclaimed folding his newspaper on his lap.

Henry was sitting in the living room of the third house they had purchased since getting married. It was big and comfortable, with a vegetable garden in the spacious backyard and a two car garage out front. For just the two of them it was ideal.

He watched as Tina put the few remaining plates in the dishwasher. She was still dressed in a simple black outfit after attending an afternoon funeral for Nick Paddington, an acquaintance of theirs. At fifty-five, she was still a striking beauty, with a body that would rival most forty-year olds.

"They took pictures," Tina said nonchalantly.

"Of what?" Henry responded, still astonished by his wife's revelation.

"Of everything."

"Even Nick? They took pictures of a dead man?"

Tina grabbed her coffee cup off the kitchen counter and proceeded into the living room where she stretched herself across the cream coloured couch. "They took shots of everyone." She gave him a stern look. "And if you had gone with me today, you would've seen that Nick looked his best."

"Yeah," Henry sneered. "Too bad he wasn't conscious to appreciate what a great job the mortician did on him." Henry flipped the paper up in front of him again.

"You shouldn't talk of the dead like that," Tina instructed while massaging her aching toes through her nylons.

"Me?" The paper came back down. Henry had a look of disbelief on his face. "I wasn't the one getting a snapshot of myself with him today was I? You might as well have been at Disney World clamouring to stand beside Goofy!"

Henry waited for her comeback. He imagined it would be something like, *Well if you were there today, Henry, I would be standing beside Goofy, wouldn't I?* But the remark never materialized. Instead, his smiling grin was greeted with a cold stare.

"You just don't understand," Tina said. "You

really had to be there to appreciate it."

Henry shook his head. "Why is it I'm the only one in this room who thinks finding picture perfect moments at a funeral is just a tad bit morbid?"

"Times change. Actually, taking the pictures was Ellen's idea."

"Well that explains how such a flaky concept originated, but what's the purpose of showing everyone dressed in black crying their eyes out?" Henry waved his hands in front of him, as if predicting the future, or suddenly seeing the next BIG THING to sweep the countryside. "What's next - your own personalized home video of the event? Maybe they could call it 'Nick's Big Day' or maybe something more appropriate - if there is such a thing." Henry's eyes widened at the possibilities. "How about 'Ashes To Ashes' - subtitled 'Say It Isn't So, Nick!'"

"That's not funny," Tina reacted.

"Neither is being blinded by a flashbulb," Henry retorted.

"They didn't use any flashes if you must know," Tina said, getting tired of explaining the new ways of life to her husband. "They were very discreet about it."

"But what's the purpose?" Henry reiterated.

Tina slumped back on the couch and took a deep breath, trying to remember exactly what she'd been told earlier. "As I was informed by Ellen's aunt, it's for spiritual release. It allows the family to visually remind themselves that they've already shed tears for their dearly departed loved one." Her voice had the quality of an interpreter haltingly decoding some foreign correspondence. "Instead, they should think about their happy times together, thus helping them to overcome the rough times in the future."

By the bewildered look on his face, it was obvious Henry hadn't gotten the full meaning of the translation. "Are you saying they're going to feel better just by looking at pictures of themselves crying? I am assuming no one is smiling in any of these candid photos."

Tina played Henry's version of what had actually transpired that afternoon over in her head. Slowly, a bit unsure of the facts herself, she agreed with him. "Well something like that."

"That's not spiritual release - it's a bizarre ritual of guilt," Henry stated, whacking his head in disbelief. "To me if you want to cry over someone you miss - then cry. Don't pull out a bunch of snaps that show you can cry. Just cry!" Henry threw up his arms in amazement. "Because if you don't, you go into denial. And when it comes to funerals there's no denying one thing: your dearly departed loved one ain't coming back!"

"You are so cold, Henry."

Henry laughed. "Not as cold as . . ."

"Don't even think of saying it," he was warned.

"You don't actually believe in that malarkey, do you?"

"I'm not saying I was totally convinced, no. But if it helps someone get over their mourning period quicker, then it's a good thing," Tina said thoughtfully. "Who knows - maybe it would've helped us through our mourning period when mother passed away," she added.

"Speak for yourself."

Tina got off the couch, walked over to Henry and punched him on the shoulder. "I can't believe you just said that," she said disgusted. "You're becoming a crude, heartless old man. I'm just glad mother isn't here to see this."

"So am I," Henry responded, kneading his muscles at the point of impact. "I just bought a new bag of cookies and you know how she could pack those babies away!" Unfortunately, he was the only one who laughed.

The death of Selma Gordon six years earlier had caused Tina to re-examine her own life. Growing up she had resented the fact her parents hadn't seen fit to provide her with a baby brother or sister. "Life would have been so much easier," she often commented. Then, with the musings of siblings and babies still racing through her mind, thoughts of their own childless marriage crept into her psyche. She still had Henry she knew, but the fact that they would depart from this world without leaving behind an heir of any kind, began to deeply trouble her. Coupled with the fact the only remaining blood relative she had was gone, Tina had become angry and depressed. Henry tried his best to understand her grief and frustration, but in light of his on-again-off-again alliance with Selma, it wasn't easy. Watching Tina staring out the bay window now, Henry could tell Nick's funeral (the first she'd attended since Selma's), had had an affect on her.

"I don't know why you could never get along with her. You know she was very supportive at the time of your accident."

"Not the hot dog story again!" Henry yelled exasperated, as he threw the paper to the floor. "I get in the only automobile accident of my life over a decade ago - and yet I'm still paying the consequences!"

"Well if you had been more careful," Tina said using her I-told-you-so tone of voice.

"I don't believe this." Henry hated it when Tina fought dirty like this, bringing up totally unrelated incidents from the past, knowing full well they'd stir up certain *unpleasant* feelings. "Someone puts muscle relaxants where there should be aspirins and it's all my fault?"

Tina turned from the window; a look of agitation on her face. "There you go again."

"There I go again what?" He knew this was going to turn ugly no matter what he said.

"Blaming others for your own actions." Tina paused for effect, which wasn't lost on Henry. "But I guess that's par for the course these days isn't it, genius?"

Henry couldn't believe how low she was attacking him. He secretly wished he could take back that 'new bag of cookies' remark somehow. Staring at Tina's smug expression only infuriated him more. "If you bring up the Fletcher deal again I'll . . ." He raised his hand slightly. His face was flush with outrage and bitterness.

"You'll what, Einstein?" Tina said taking a few steps toward him. "Throw a fit? Storm out of the room? Call me by my mother's name?" She shook her head. "I know you wouldn't dare hit me."

"There's always a first time for everything," he remarked with a smirk.

Tina brushed by him, full of confidence. "Ah, you're all hot air," she said, dismissing his threats with a wave of her hand. "Because you know if you ever tried, *ever* tried, it wouldn't be long before I was buying film for your funeral!" She let out a laugh at the idea.

"You wouldn't dare," Henry said horrified by her insinuation.

Tina walked to the bedroom to change into something more comfortable.

"Actually, instead of film I'd probably go for your video concept," she yelled back at Henry, stringing him along, savouring every syllable. "That way I could replay it over and over again to enjoy the fact you're there, but not really there. Sleeping, but not snoring." Her tone turned to one of amusement. "It would also be the only testament to the fact you could keep your mouth shut for longer than sixty seconds!"

Henry repositioned himself in the recliner. "Oh, aren't you funny," he said sarcastically, not caring if she heard his comment or not. "Funny looking maybe."

Upon re-entering the living room, dressed in her blue tracksuit, Tina sat down on the sofa and started to survey one of her many design magazines - the ones she insisted added class to the coffee table. She knew it would be awhile for Henry - who was deep into his newspaper - to cool down and begin talking to her again.

Fifteen minutes passed.

"Do you have a picture from Nick's funeral?" Henry asked, his voice casual, but with just a tinge of curiosity to it.

"Maybe," Tina replied, not looking up from her magazine.

"Well let me see it then."

"Why - so you could laugh at me crying?"

Their eyes finally met.

"You were actually crying?" Henry asked, stunned by her comment.

"It's like a wedding really," Tina said remembering the day's events.

"Except the groom isn't going to show, right?" Henry chuckled at his joke. Tina didn't. Instead she continued her comparison.

"Would you please shut up," she demanded. Tina waited for Henry to get control of himself before going on. "It's like a wedding because you get caught up in the drama of the thing. Seeing the bride coming down the aisle fills people with joy and happiness. You can't help but get excited. At a funeral the same thing happens."

"You got excited?" Henry asked.

Tina ignored the remark. "No - you get sad. The poor lady beside me was Nick's secretary and she wept through the entire service."

"Maybe he stiffed her on her last pay cheque. Or didn't give her his two weeks notice." Henry was trying his best to retain his self-control. "Hey, maybe she was crying because she couldn't believe they were taking so many pictures of her boss. Did they get a good one of her?"

"You're impossible!" Tina pronounced, frustrated by Henry's insensitivity. "I'm trying to tell you about my day - a day they buried a friend of ours - and all you seem to care about is yourself and preserving the myth that you're remotely funny. Well let me tell you something Shecky - you're not funny and neither is your lack of interest in what I do or what happens to me. All you care about is your high class clients." Tina's voice had risen in tiny increments with each sentence. By now she was screaming at him with full force. "But they don't make your bed or fix your meals! And I'm quite certain none of those stuffed shirts would be caught dead cleaning your underwear!"

"Are you through?" Henry asked, thinking this was merely an extension of the 'new bag of cookies' argument. For once in a long time, Henry was mistaken. In reality, he had no idea what the real truth was behind Tina's stinging remarks. However, she was about to bring him up to date.

"Am I through? Is that what you just said?" Henry could see the contempt in Tina's eyes and felt immediately uncomfortable. "The answer is No - but why don't we run our marriage like a corporation? You know the ones – thirty-five years and out, whether you like it or not. Well come next month my time may very well be up and I'll have to go and find another equally useless executive to take care of. Hey, I know - maybe Edward Fletcher is looking for some help."

"That was low, Tina, even for you." Henry got out of his chair throwing his paper onto an end table. Rage registered on his face. "But on second thought, it was merely typical of you. The fact is Edward Fletcher screwed me over - not the other way around!" he stated emphatically.

"Blaming others again are you?" Tina said coolly.

"Sometimes the truth is the only thing standing in the way of justice," Henry countered self-righteously.

"And what is that supposed to mean, Sherlock?"

"Only that the truth in the Fletcher deal hasn't come to light yet."

"But when it does - you'll be cleared of all wrong doing? And what if everyone believes Fletcher's version of the truth over yours? What then - you'll blame everyone else, making it into a huge conspiracy?"

"You don't know what you're talking about."

In her heart, Tina knew that certainly was the truth, but she also realized something more than just a sour advertising deal had fallen through. Not since Henry opened his own agency, had Tina seen him so frazzled and edgy. It had been going on for about a month now and with each passing week Tina felt more and more isolated from Henry and his work. They rarely discussed business anymore. In fact, they rarely had any type of meaningful conversations of late, which brought Tina to the sneaking suspicion Henry may have been having an affair. Deep down though, she knew it couldn't happen. As she had watched them bury Nick this afternoon, she had made up her mind to get to the bottom of things tonight. Life was just too short, she concluded.

"Maybe that's because you rarely talk to me anymore," she began forcibly. "In the beginning of our marriage, you held no secrets from me. If you were in trouble at work, you'd tell me. We'd discuss it and if things were going great we'd share the joy together. But not now. Now everything is a big secret, isn't it?" She glared at him coldly. "I started hearing about your problems from the newspapers, Henry. Do you know how that made me feel? Do you even care? You come home these days and lock yourself in the study, shutting me out like I'm some kid who's unable to understand the pressures of being an adult."

"I don't mean to make you feel that way, but . . ." Henry was cut off in mid-apology.

"But what?" Tina asked, still combative. "You think if you tell me what's really wrong, that I'll snap under the weight of it all? Did I become deranged when we lost the baby? No. Did I go insane when we almost lost the house trying to set up your business? No. And just for good measure, did I go mad when you had your heart scare two years ago? No. And do you know why?"

"No," Henry said preparing for another assault on his senses. "But I'm sure you're going to tell me."

Tina got up and started to walk around the room, turning to face Henry, every once in awhile, as if to emphasize her anger with him. “I’ll tell you. It’s because I love you! Your problems are my problems. Your triumphs are my triumphs. Why can’t you understand that? Don’t you remember our wedding vows: ‘For better or worse. For richer or poorer. In sickness and in health. ‘Til death do us part’? Don’t you remember - or are you so wrapped up in your own business world, that you’ve forgotten about our little world together?” Tears of frustration began to well up in Tina’s eyes. “I’m not sure anymore, Henry.”

“You wouldn’t understand, Tina,” Henry said trying to reassure her. “Honest.”

“Try me,” she demanded. “That’s all I’m asking. Even if I don’t grasp all the finer points, I might be able to help you figure out the big picture.” She inhaled deeply, trying to calm down. “That’s all I really want to do - just help. And to feel wanted again.”

Henry knew he had hurt Tina’s confidence in herself, and in him, over the past few weeks. He was ashamed of himself, but in a way felt as though he had to protect her as best he could.

“I don’t want to involve you. It’s bad enough I have to live with what I’ve done without you worrying about it too.”

His voice was impassioned, which both infuriated and reassured Tina. “Henry, nothing you can say or anything you’ve done can surprise me.” A slight smile came over her face. “I realized that a long time ago. So give me a try. I promise not to get upset."

Henry thought it over. He knew although she sounded sincere, it could be a trick. To tell or not to tell her? That was the question. Faced with this Catch-22 situation, he simply shrugged his shoulders and blurted it out.

"Okay fine. In a nutshell: we're not only broke, but I think I'm about to be arrested for insider trading."

His voice was flat and unemotional. Tina's was not.

"*We're WHAT?*" she screamed. "*You think you're going to be WHAT?*"

"It was all a misunderstanding. I swear," Henry said in his own defence.

Tina came at him. "Don't you blame this one on anyone else, Mister! Not this time."

Why did I tell her? Henry asked himself. "I knew you wouldn't understand, let alone not get angry."

Tina stood a foot away from him now, her eyes fiery. "You're going to be a love slave to a guy named Snake while I'm left here with no money to live on - and I shouldn't be upset? From where I stand I'll be getting the raw end of the deal. At least you'll have three meals a day and someone to snuggle up to at night!"

"Could you get serious?" Henry said in the same flat unemotional tone he'd used earlier.

"Who says I'm not?" Tina countered. Raising her hand to Henry's chest he was afraid she was going to hit him again. Instead she gave him a push backwards, sending him sprawling further back into his recliner. "This is very traumatic for me you know." Annoyance coupled with sheer fury dripped off each word. "It's not every day a wife discovers her husband is a complete moron. On second thought, maybe that happens all the time. Maybe that's why the divorce rate hovers around 50%. It has nothing to do with adultery or kids or toothpaste caps - it's a direct consequence of discovering your spouse is a duffus!"

Tina turned her back on Henry, whose eyes appeared to be filled with terror. *She's gone mad,* he thought as she continued to ponder her last observation.

"I wonder if the government knows about this? They probably do, but if they exposed it there'd be a rash of broken engagements and marriages, which in turn means fewer family taxes, which would ultimately send the country to the verge of collapse. And for what?" She turned her full attention back to Henry who hadn't flinched a muscle since her verbal assault had begun. "Because men think they're so good at being providers. Well it just isn't so - as you're undoubtably about to prove to me!"

Henry squirmed uneasily in his chair, trying to regain an ounce of composure before speaking again. "Are you through?" he asked tentatively.

"A more appropriate question would be - are we?"

"Well . . . not as of yet," he professed optimistically.

This of course enraged Tina. "And what does that mean?" She stared at him as he tried to formulate an appropriate answer. "Do I have enough time to go on one more wild shopping spree before everything we own is repossessed? Actually . . ." She tapped her index finger on her lips. "Maybe I'll wait until they truck all this old stuff away. That way I can start over fresh."

"And where exactly would you get the money from, lovey?"

When Henry talked sarcastically about the availability of funds, Tina knew he wasn't joking around. This was more serious than she had imagined she concluded, slumping onto the couch. But there must be *some* money left over.

"Our credit cards?" she ventured.

"Already at their limits," Henry said, almost amused somehow by the critical financial situation he had gotten them into.

"Our bank account then?" Tina said hopefully.

"Think again."

"The coin collection?"

"Cashed in."

"The cars?" A worried, childlike look began to creep across Tina's lovely face.

"Virtually up on blocks as we speak."

"My piggy bank?" she said despondently, knowing in her heart that Henry had somehow lost everything. *Why did I marry this idiot?* she thought.

"I'm afraid that little piggy already went to market." Henry tried to stifle a smile but was not successful. "The stock market that is."

"Then what's left?" she shrieked. "What do I have to bargain with?" A brilliant plan suddenly formed in her head. "I know," she said excitedly. "What about our life insurance?"

Henry raised an eyebrow. "That's only good to you if I were to die."

"Yeah? And?"

"Well I don't plan to kick off for some time yet," he stated.

"Leave the planning to me, buddy," Tina replied deviously.

Henry stood from his chair, only after deciding that his barracuda of a wife had calmed down - or at least had given up sufficiently to continue their discussion cordially.

"We're not as bad off as it seems, Tina," he proposed.

"No, it's worse." She glanced down at her left hand. "After the trial all I'll have left of our marriage is this diamond ring."

"Now's probably not the best time to tell you this, but it's not really a diamond. It's glass," Henry said casually.

"What?"

Seeing her wild reaction, Henry laughed. "I was kidding. Lighten up, will you?" Tina continued to stare daggers at him. "And I'm telling the truth about not being so bad off. Who knows - by tomorrow everything could be straightened out."

Tina scoffed at the suggestion. "And maybe North America could survive a recreational game of nuclear war with a developing country, run by an insane military dictator!"

"Look, Tina, here are the facts," Henry started to say, as he sat beside her on the couch. She automatically moved away from him a couple of inches. "First of all, tomorrow our funds and property will be temporarily frozen by some government agency, as they try to figure out just what Fletcher & Associates were trying to pull. Secondly, my impending arrest may or may not even occur. It's really just a nasty rumour going around. And thirdly, I haven't done anything wrong. Honest."

Tina wasn't buying his sob story for a second. The fact he had even been involved in a situation that would lead to such circumstances though, wasn't what was bothering her. "Oh you've done plenty wrong," she said glancing into his hopeful, sincere looking face. "You seem to have forgotten this is a partnership and I don't remember giving you permission to gamble our life savings on some idiotic stock hunch."

Henry was about to utter a quick reply but suddenly thought better of it. "Not in so many words . . ." he finally declared.

"What?" Tina was not about to play the fall guy.

"Well . . . all I've ever heard is how we don't have enough money - or that we can't travel more. So . . ."

He was abruptly cut off by Tina who pointed an accusing finger at him.

"Oh no you don't! Don't put this on my

shoulders. I've always wanted you to succeed. There's never been any doubt about that. But at any or all cost? Don't be ridiculous. What's the use of losing what we already have?"

Henry tried valiantly to refute her comment. "What about your 'Nothing ventured, nothing gained' theory?"

"You call everything we've built over thirty-five years nothing?" Tina retaliated as she surveyed the well furnished living room.

"No, but if it's the only thing to venture with . . ." Henry knew his arguments weren't worth the paper those bad stocks had been printed on.

"You don't see it, do you?" A determined expression to bring this futile debate to a conclusion appeared on Tina's face. "Our house, our life savings, cars - everything - is not part of some fantasy Monopoly game. In the version you seem to be playing, when you go to jail, all you'll need is to roll doubles to get out!"

"Monopoly is such a stupid game," Henry said shaking his head.

"And how would you know?" Tina said mockingly. "How many times have you actually won at it?"

"I don't know. Five maybe six times."

Tina laughed - almost barked at him in ridicule. "Well I'll tell you, Mr. High Roller. Mr. High Finance."

I was certain you would, Henry thought.

"The fact is you've never won. Not a single game," Tina's voice rang out victoriously.

"What about the time we played with your mother and her friend Edith?"

"What about it? You made us play until four in the morning! Edith narrowly missed losing an eye when her head fell on Park Place due to sheer exhaustion!"

Henry, remembering the sight of Edith's collapse at the kitchen table, began to laugh uncontrollably. "It took us a full five minutes to extract that one house from her left nostril! It was a good thing I hadn't put those hotels on yet!"

Tina tried to suppress her amusement of that night. "You're lucky she didn't file a lawsuit against us," she said chuckling slightly.

Tears cascaded down Henry's cheeks as his body rocked with laughter. "Even if she could - what would she claim? That I put those houses too close to the side of the board, knowing full well at sometime during the evening she'd just zonk out and impale her nose with a game piece? Sounds kind of far fetched, doesn't it?" Henry doubled over in stitches.

"It wasn't funny at the time," Tina reminded him, regaining her poise.

"Speak for yourself. I had to leave the room I was laughing so hard!"

"I'll remember that when the federal agents come to the door with a warrant for your arrest."

Henry's spirited convulsions slowly began to die down, brought back to reality by Tina's statement. "There you go killing the laughter again."

"I'm sorry to be such a party pooper. I just don't find our present situation all that humorous,"

Tina said bleakly.

"Yeah, but I bet if we were a million dollars richer today, the only laughing you'd be doing is on the way to the bank," Henry asserted.

"At the moment, that's a very large 'IF'. In fact, it's so large in size as to become one of those fishing tales. You know - the one that got away type." Tina shook her head in amazement. "In our case though, we're not only going to lose the rod, but the boat, the tackle and the cooler! And if we're not careful we'll end up so far underwater, we may never see or feel dry land again!"

Henry knew what his wife was saying was the truth. Still he felt things could somehow work out for them. Although, he hadn't a clue how.

"Could you stop being so pessimistic?"

Tina shot him a cold look, but soon her features began to soften. "I'd like to think of it as being realistic - with just a hint of hysteria. I just can't believe you let this go so far for so long without telling me about it."

A show of guilt broadcast from Henry's face. Even his posture emitted sole fault for what had happened.

"I just couldn't." As his eyes met Tina's, Henry knew it was time to come clean. He owed her that much, if not a great deal more. As he began his tale of misfortune and stupidity, his tone conveyed a sense of excitement, like that of a young boy who desperately wants his parents to believe that the trouble he now found himself in was really the result of good intentions gone wrong.

"For the first time in my life, I thought I had actually made the big time," Henry began. "That I had actually been given my one big break. This was it, Tina! It was the fulfillment of all our dreams. When Fletcher left my office a month ago telling me to buy his stock before he sold out to Hammersmith, I couldn't believe it. I knew that stock would go from $30 to at least $130 a share, in one day! How was I to know he was pitching the same line to all the advertising executives in town? It was perfect. His stock hit the roof, as everyone jumped on the bandwagon and he knew no one could say a thing because of insider trading regulations. Now we're told the stock is worthless and Fletcher is threatening bankruptcy."

"Leaving all you poor saps out to dry."

"Bingo." He looked at Tina, trying to detect if she believed him or not.

"So you think you gambled big and lost big, right?" was all she said.

"I know I did," Henry replied shamefully. "The only way I could get our money back and not go to jail is by some miracle."

Tina smiled. "And what if just such a hypothetical miracle did occur - what would be the first thing you'd do?"

"I'm not sure."

"Maybe take your loving, understanding wife to an expensive dinner and a show?" Tina suggested innocently.

"Maybe but . . ."

"Or how about taking a vacation on the

French Riviera or somewhere equally appealing?"

"Sure," Henry agreed whole-heartily. What did he have to lose? "Why don't we just say I'll take you to a show and dinner on the Riviera? Would you like that?" Tina nodded. "How about a mink or maybe a whole new wardrobe? Sound interesting?" Tina nodded again. "And while we're at it - why don't we just sign up for one of those trips to the moon NASA keeps promising? Or better yet - and this would be the topper - why not have our bodies frozen when we die? That way when they find a cure for whatever ailed us, they could bring us back so we could continue to argue with each other for another thirty-five years!"

Tina considered the various proposals set in front of her. "The Riviera and the mink are tempting. As for being frozen though . . . I think one lifetime of bickering with you is sufficient. Wouldn't you agree?"

"I was just thinking of hypothetical situations, dear."

"But you would do these things for me . . . if you could?" For the first time since their argument had erupted, Tina inched closer to Henry on the couch.

"Of course, I would. I love you. I never meant for any of this to happen."

"Hey, who does?" Tina shrugged.

As she began to put her arms around his neck, Henry was overcome with emotion; relieved everything was finally out in the open. "The fact remains, Tina," he said lovingly, "that I could lose every material thing in the world and I wouldn't care. Just as long as I still had you by my side."

Suddenly Tina was no longer by his side but up and walking into the kitchen.

"Boy, you're dumber than I thought - not that I don't appreciate what you're saying or anything," she said sarcastically. "But if there's one thing worse than having to listen to a stupid man, it's having to listen to one beg for forgiveness. So let's just end this okay? Open this up. It came this morning while you were sulking in the study."

From the microwave cart Tina produced a white envelope. She threw it onto Henry's lap. He opened it readily.

"You kept this from me all day?" he said astonished by her deception.

"Yep," she laughed.

He continued to read the contents of his lawyer's letter as he spoke. "You let me suffer like this, knowing full well the feds were going solely after Fletcher and not going to pursue a case against me?" Tina nodded with a smirk. "It also says here if I did decide to co-operate with them, that they'd grant me full immunity."

Tina grabbed the letter from his hands and scanned the page.

"Immunity? I must have misread that part. I thought it said immunization. I was hoping they were going to give you some kind of shot - putting you out of my misery!"

"How could you be so insensitive as to keep this from me?" Henry asked incensed.

"Hey look here, you would be Wall Street Wiener," she said raising her voice slightly. "You're just lucky I'm showing you tonight. By tomorrow morning, I could have gotten a new car and a full-time houseboy out of you! You got off easy from where I stand."

Henry chuckled nervously. "You're not going to hold me to those silly promises, are you?"

"Only the good ones," Tina said gleefully.

"You're insane," Henry howled. "Even with this letter we still haven't the money to even go to the store - let alone France!"

Tina again went to the microwave cart and produced a second envelope. From it, she pulled out a cheque and waved it in front of Henry's confused face.

"Oh, didn't I tell you? A pimply faced office boy from Fletcher & Associates dropped this off for you this morning. It reimburses you for everything you invested - plus interest." She folded the small piece of paper, pulled out her sweat shirt and pushed the cheque into her bra. "Now, I'm not normally in the habit of taking hush money . . . but in this case I thought, Ah what the heck."

Henry sat still in his chair, dumbfounded by Tina's revelations. "You are getting to be too deceitful for your own good old woman."

"I don't like the word old," she replied, grinning ear to ear. "Mature is much more appropriate I should think."

"What would I do without you?" Henry asked.

"Who cares - as long as I was having fun!"

"Well, speaking of fun - what would you like to do tonight, before we jet off to Europe with the proceeds from that cheque?"

Tina thought it over carefully.

"Let's play Monopoly."

"Are you serious?" She shook her head in agreement. "I would have thought you'd had enough of playing high risk games of chance after today."

"Well as per usual, you are wrong," she said firmly. "I'll get the box from the closet." As she stepped by Henry, she suddenly stopped and grabbed him by the shirt. "And one more thing: If you ever pull a stunt like this again . . . I'll warn you right now that it won't be a pretty picture."

"Okay, okay."

"Oh and speaking of pictures." Tina walked for a third time to the microwave stand and grabbed a snapshot, which she handed to Henry as she walked out of the room. "Nick sends his best."

Henry stared at the picture and read the inscription on the front. "Wish you were here? He certainly does have a grave sense of humour, doesn't he?" Henry called out.

"He certainly does," Tina yelled back.

Looking more closely at the picture Henry said, "At least where you are, Nick old boy, you don't have a nagging wife hanging around you 24 hours a day."

Tina suddenly re-appeared in the doorway, startling Henry.

"I heard that!"

"But you didn't let me finish, dear," Henry stammered, looking to Nick for some inspiration. "I was about to tell Nick here how lucky he was, as now he'd know how I feel living with you each and every day."

Tina walked over to where Henry was standing - a sheepish grin spread across his lips.

"Nice save, eh?" he said, leaning forward to kiss her.

"Not bad, Romeo. Not bad at all."

CHAPTER FIVE

"Forever Love"

****

The day was perfect: not a cloud in the sky, no humidity, and with the temperature hovering in the mid-seventies. In all, it was an excellent day for jogging.

Since their sixty-fifth birthdays, Tina and Henry had tried to get out of the house once a day for a quick run around the neighbourhood. That was going on five years ago now. It gave them something to look forward to and some quality time together. After they'd retired, it seemed they saw less of each other than when they were working full-time. Tina had her knitting and stained glass classes twice a week, while Henry partook in more "manly" pastimes such as senior's baseball (as the star first baseman) and weight lifting at a local gym. Although society had deemed them old, they were still very much young at heart.

"You can't beat a day like today," Henry observed.

"You always say that."

"Well, it's true. Clean air. Sun in the sky. No

dogs barking." Turning the corner Henry paused for a moment before he started to add, "You know . . ."

"That it's just like this in Florida," Tina said laughing, doing her best imitation of him.

"Have I said that too many times?" Henry asked sheepishly.

"You said that too many times back in 1990, Mr. Cole," Tina smiled.

"Well!" Henry said huffily. "I'm sorry I've bored you with my petty conversation for forty years, Mrs. Cole."

"What about the ten years before that?" Tina shot back.

"I honestly don't remember our first ten years together. I was too much in love," Henry quipped sweetly.

Tina gave him an evil look. "And if I ever find out who she was - we're through!"

The light they had been waiting for finally changed and they started across the street.

"Huh!" Henry exclaimed as their house came into sight. "You couldn't kick me out, old woman."

"And why's that?"

"Because you haven't any strength left in your legs - that's why!"

"You don't think so?" Tina said challenging him.

"I know so."

"We'll just see about that. Last one to the front porch is an old coot!"

Immediately Tina pulled away from Henry racing toward the house. Henry, who was totally taken aback by her speed, languished a few yards behind.

"You think you're pretty smart, don't you?" he yelled.

Tina glanced quickly over her shoulder. "As you can see from your vantage point - I do appear to be ahead of you, Mister."

"Oh ya?"

Henry was not about to finish in second place. Summoning all his will power - and what strength he still had remaining in his legs - he sped past Tina in one final burst of acceleration. As he bounded up the porch steps, he was oblivious to the fact Tina had stopped running and was now clutching her chest.

At the top of the steps, Henry jubilantly raised his arms in victory. "Winner and still champeeeen . . . Henry . . ." The word 'Cole' stuck in his throat as he turned to see Tina fall to her knees. His smile completely disappeared, as did the colour in his face. "Tina? My Tina! What's wrong?" he cried rushing to her side.

Tina's eyes were still alert, still sparkling with enthusiasm when he reached her. As Henry held her in his arms she appeared to want to say something. Anything. But then fear slowly began to show on her face.

"Just hold on, Tina. Whatever it is will pass," Henry said, as tears began to form in his eyes. "Everything will be all right." Henry briefly looked to the beautiful sky overhead. "Please God help us."

His appeal for divine intervention seemed to stir Tina briefly. Her eyes looked past Henry's terror stricken face to the blue sky above them. A faint smile came over her features, but she was still unable to speak to her husband.

"Oh, Tina, my love," Henry sobbed, pulling her close to his chest. "Please don't leave me. I need you so much. Please don't go. Not yet." The sense of dread he had been experiencing, suddenly turned to anger. "Don't take her – take me!" he yelled to the heavens. "Take me! She can still do so much here. I can't."

Under normal circumstances Henry would wait for a snappy comment from Tina, like, *Oh, stop feeling sorry for yourself, you old fool,* or *Do you really think if given the choice between you and me, God would pick you? In your dreams, buster.*

These were no normal circumstances, however.

Knowing her time was indeed precious, Tina struggled to whisper a final message to her partner of fifty years.

"I'll never leave you, Henry. I'll . . . always be near."

As the words faded, so too did Tina's expression. Her eyes closed slowly. Realizing she was truly gone, Henry held her tightly, no longer trying to hold back his grief.

"I love you, Tina. I'll always love you."

As he gently kissed her forehead, he could hear a neighbour shouting that she'd called for help. But there on the front lawn of the house they had called home for over thirty five years, Henry knew only the good Lord could help Tina now.

****

The funeral was a simple affair. Years before, each of them had written out plans for what they wanted. Henry followed Tina's instructions to the letter. The group of mourners was a collection of neighbours, friends and people they had worked with before retiring to the so-called good life. The service was held in the same church they had been married in. Remarkably the minister who had performed that ceremony - who was the same age as the Coles, having just graduated from bible college at the time - also took part in this service.

The day was much like it had been three days earlier: sunny and warm. At the cemetery Henry stood at the side of the open grave clutching a single white carnation in his hands as Rev. Snow said a few final words.

"She was a woman of many strengths and devoted to not only her husband Henry, but also to various organizations for which she volunteered. This earth will sadly miss the presence of Tina Cole. We often say that all good things must come to an end. For Tina, her journey is just beginning. She is now residing in her new heavenly home and is starting to experience the joys of life in paradise, with its overwhelming feelings of love and happiness. Things that we can only hope to see when the Lord calls us to Him. And as long as we never forget the caring person that Tina Cole was, she will never truly leave us. She will always be near."

Hearing this phrase, Henry looked up from the carnation remembering his wife's dying words. As the casket began its slow decent into the ground, Henry stepped forward and placed the flower on top of the casket. As Rev. Snow began to pray, everyone bowed their heads.

"Our heavenly Father - as we give to you Tina Cole to love and care for, please help each and every one of us to remain strong during this time of sudden sadness. And be with us in our times of need, especially with Tina's devoted husband Henry. In your name we ask this. Amen."

The mourners repeated "Amen" with the Reverend and began to mingle awkwardly as they made their way back to their cars. A few remained standing with Henry, who tried to keep his composure intact. As a single tear fell down his cheek, he whispered "I love you, Tina," before reluctantly turning to walk away.

****

The service and the traditional get together afterward had gone off without any problems. One of Henry's worries was that Ellen Faber would appear out of nowhere with a flash camera. Thankfully she never made an appearance. Those who did return to the house sipped coffee and ate the assorted sandwiches offered, while sharing entertaining stories about Tina. Maxie Harper told everyone of the time she and Tina had been stopped by a policeman the previous year on the way to the mall. When asked by the officer if she knew she was speeding, Tina quickly replied, "Of course I do. But at our age it's better to get there today than to wait until tomorrow for our rheumatism to flare up again!" The officer laughed and let them go.

Stanley Bender remembered asking her for a date when they were teenagers. "Of course she turned me down," he laughed. "She wasn't looking for a smart, handsome, athletic type like me - she was looking for someone like old Henry here!" Everyone laughed. Even Henry laughed - he was used to being the butt of jokes, especially when Tina was in the room. Regardless if they were alone or if there were twenty people milling around, she would always send a few zingers his way. Of course he sent his share back. It was like their marriage was a constant game of one-up-manship without a clear winner ever being established. And if there was no winner, it meant there was no loser either. That was the whole object of the game in the first place.

After an hour of lively chit chat and laughter, the small group of close friends that remained raised their glasses in one final toast to the late, great Tina Cole.

"To our dear friend, Tina," Andy Sommer began. "We were lucky to know you and cherished you dearly. May you rest in peace, always." His gaze turned to Henry who looked longingly at their wedding picture over the fireplace. "And one more thing, Tina, keep an eye on your good husband Henry here. You're the only one in this room who can keep up with him. Cheers." The glasses were brought together, with everyone allowing a final pleasant thought to pass through their mind in regards to their recently departed friend.

Soon, all but Linda King, a neighbour in her mid-fifties, had left - with each person giving Henry some form of advice and maybe a hug on their way out. "Keep in touch if you need anything," they all echoed.

"Now are you sure you're going to be okay, Henry?" Linda asked as Henry held her coat. "Because if you aren't . . ."

"I'll be fine, Linda," Henry cut in. "It's just with the funeral and then all the people coming here, I haven't had time to just sit down and think. With peace and quiet in the house, I can do that now."

The smile on his face comforted her. Pulling on her coat, Linda hugged him. "Just don't think too much," she whispered.

"I'll try not to."

Breaking her embrace, Henry took a few steps to the door and opened it. Like all the others, she also gave him one last piece of advice.

"And if it gets too quiet for you, don't hesitate to call Ted and me next door."

"I don't think that will be necessary, but thanks anyhow."

"Okay then. Now I'll drop by tomorrow with some lunch for you."

"I look forward to it," Henry said with a mild laugh. "You better get home to Ted before he starts to worry about you." Henry watched Linda as she started down the front steps and added, "Good night and . . . thanks."

"I'll be by around noon," Linda called back.

"I'll be here."

That night around 9:30, Henry slowly looked up at the long stairway in front of him. At the top of the steps was the master bedroom - the one room in the house where Henry and Tina had always discussed their innermost hopes and fears for five decades. And although he had slept alone for the past two evenings, tonight would be different. After today's funeral the realization that Tina was truly gone was no longer in doubt.

After shutting out all the lights downstairs, Henry's first thought was to sleep in the guest room. He really didn't think he could handle sleeping in their bed - at least not for this one particular night. But as he pulled the covers down on the spare bed, he felt guilty. It was as if he was turning his back on Tina. Sleeping in this unfamiliar room for just one night could very well become a habit.

"You're a giant coward, Henry Cole," he chastised himself walking down the hall to their bedroom. "She may be dead but she surely isn't gone."

As he entered the room a gentle, cool night breeze fluttered the bedroom's thin white curtains. Thinking that the last thing he needed was a cold, Henry closed the window and then climbed into the queen-sized bed. Only now it felt like a king-sized one. Before pulling up the covers Henry reached for the lamp on the night table. His action was halted as he saw Tina staring back at him. It was one of the nicest pictures he had ever taken of her. In it she was full of life, smiling and laughing at him - at the world. And best of all, it was shot only a few short weeks earlier. It was the Tina he would always remember.

"Good night, Tina. I love you."

Every night for the past half century he had awaited her reply. Tonight he wished he could have heard her say just one last time, *I love you too, Henry.* As the silence enveloped him, he reached for the lamp and flicked it off.

Lying there in the dark, he came to the heartbreaking conclusion that yes, he was now all alone.

****

The clock on Tina's night table read three o'clock in the morning. Curled up on his half of the bed Henry slept a troubled sleep. The covers were wrapped around him, pulled out of the end of the bed (something he used to complain to Tina for doing), which ensured that his feet would get ice cold at some point during the night. Outside a car horn honked not once, but three times. It was this commotion (coupled with his cold feet) that awoke Henry.

Blurry eyed he looked about the room. Everything still seemed to be in order. But there was one thing that puzzled him. "I thought I closed that window," he muttered to himself. Quickly he untangled himself from the sheets and started toward the half opened window.

"Oh please don't shut it, Henry. You know

how I loved the breeze at night."

Henry froze in mid-stride. The voice had come from behind him and he didn't dare look back, frightened by what he might encounter.

"Who are you?" he ventured, still looking toward the open window. "What do you want?"

"Boy - I've been gone just three short days and he can't even remember who I am!" the voice exclaimed.

Henry very slowly turned to face his uninvited intruder. What he saw took his breath away. There sitting gingerly on the corner of the bed was Tina, or at least a faint outline of Tina. She was wearing a bluish coloured gown and looked absolutely luminous.

"I'm now glad we didn't have children," the image continued. "When they'd come home from college each summer, you'd probably treat them like total strangers!"

Her laugh was unmistakable. Henry risked a few steps toward her. "You look like Tina Cole. And you talk like Tina Cole. But she's dead. I mean you were . . . we held the funeral for her today."

Watching her husband stammer away broke Tina's heart. "I know, Henry," she said softly. "Thank you for the flower." Henry hadn't noticed until then that in her left hand Tina held a solitary white carnation. "White carnations were always my favourites."

"But how?" Henry said, still not trusting his eyes. "You know . . ."

"That I am here with you now?" Henry nodded his head. "Well I'm really not sure myself.

I don't even know how long I can stay or if once I leave I can ever come back."

For a moment Henry stared at his wife in disbelief before taking a spot beside her on the bed. "But there's so much I want to tell you," he said. "And I don't want you to leave me without a warning again - like you did out there on the lawn."

"Oh, Henry," Tina replied lovingly. "I didn't want to go. But I had no choice."

"I should have let you win that race!" Henry said bitterly. "It was all my fault. I should have known your heart couldn't take that kind of stress."

Henry was close to tears, but wouldn't let Tina look into his eyes.

"At the time, you bet it was my legs that couldn't stand the pressure," she said with a smile. "Remember?"

"But you didn't have a leg cramp!" Henry cried out defensively. "You had a heart attack!" He finally allowed Tina to see his face; it was red with anger and sadness. "When I turned around and saw you on the lawn I almost died."

"How do you think I felt?" Tina said with a laugh. "I did die!"

"How can you joke about this?" Henry exclaimed.

"Who's joking? I did die you know."

It was like they had never parted company. The light ribbing, the jokes, the tone of the conversation - it was like it had always been. It was like old times.

"You know what I mean," Henry said calming down.

"Of course I know what you mean, Henry," Tina reassured him. "I've always known what you meant. Like the first time you asked me out." Tina floated off the bed and hovered in front of Henry. "You said, 'Tina - would you like to go get something to drink?' Do you remember that?"

The sight of his wife levitating before him was at first unsettling, but as the seconds passed it seemed like the most natural thing in the world.

"You were the prettiest girl at that beach," Henry recalled tenderly.

"That's the way I remember it too!" Tina said, a big smile coming over her face. "But anyhow . . . when you asked me to go for that drink, I knew right then what you were really trying to say was, 'I think I've just fallen in love with you, Tina Gordon. Would you spend the rest of your life with me?'"

"And that's why you went out with me?"

"Of course not, you old fool! I was just really thirsty that day!"

"That's not how I remember it."

"Oh is that so?"

"I may have fallen into your lap that afternoon, but you had your eye on me well before then. I think you even had a huge crush on me."

"Well let me tell you something, Mister - you were misinformed." Tina effortlessly made her way to the window. "I don't know who would tell you such things about me."

"Mary Lynn Gustenburg."

"Why that little . . ."

"Better be careful what you say, Tina," Henry

interrupted her. "Mary Lynn passed away a few years ago. Who knows - maybe you'll bump into her again . . . up there." Henry looked toward the ceiling.

"So what exactly are you saying?" Tina asked following her husband's gaze. "That I should respect the dead?"

"You know more about that subject just now then I do, dear," Henry said submissively.

Tina laughed. "And don't you forget it!"

Henry watched his wife's ghostly form for a moment. Even in death she looked so alive. More alive than most of their friends he concluded. As she stood by the window, he noticed that the curtains swayed with the incoming breeze but the bottom of Tina's gown didn't. The wind was passing right through her, like she wasn't really there at all. This realization sent shivers down Henry's spine. What if she wasn't really here? What if all the love he felt for her right then was a dream of some kind? Before total panic could paralyze him, Tina again asserted herself into his psyche. Dead or alive, awake or asleep, she was still very much with him in the room, he thought.

"I wonder if I'm still married to you since I passed on?" Tina asked quizzically.

"You'll always be Mrs. Henry Cole!" Henry proclaimed. "And don't you let any of those angels tell you differently! You're mine until the end of time."

"But what about our wedding vows?" Tina playfully inquired. "It states very clearly, 'til death do us part."

"So?"

"So, I guess that you're free of all marital obligations to me." Tina looked in Henry's direction. Just as he was about to respond she asked him another question. "You wouldn't remarry would you, Henry?"

"Hmmm . . . let me think for a sec," Henry started. "I guess if the opportunity arose I would have to at least consider it, wouldn't I?"

"Henry Cole!"

"Gotcha."

"You had better be kidding," she said with authority. "I didn't sacrifice fifty years of my life putting up with your nonsense, only to see you marry again after I'm dead and gone." Tina pondered that thought. "Which I guess would be right now."

Henry could tell that even in death his wife's emotions still ran deep. "You needn't worry about me. I've had more love in my lifetime than one man deserves."

"And there were times, Henry, when I thought I had enough love in me for two men."

"And if I had ever found out who that other guy was . . . I would have . . ." Henry clutched his hand into a fist.

"You'd have cleaned his clock?" Tina said with a smile.

"Maybe."

"At your age, you're lucky to wind your watch!" Tina laughed. "So don't waste your time on other people's clocks, okay?"

"Deal," Henry said, returning her grin.

The breeze again made the curtains sway gently back and forth, but not Tina's gown.

"What is it like, Tina? You know - up there."

Tina looked into her husband's face; it reminded her of a young boy's. "Oh Henry, it's wonderful - simply wonderful," she began. "Of course I haven't seen very much of it yet, but what I have seen is more beautiful than anything I ever saw here on Earth." Tina glanced toward the window. "The colours are more vibrant. The bird's songs are sweeter. The air is crystal clean and smells like a fresh spring morning."

"Have you met anyone else?" Henry ventured cautiously. "Maybe someone I used to know."

"Like your father perhaps?"

"My mother or my father."

Since the age of fifteen, Henry had been an orphan. His parents had died in a freak automobile accident while taking a weekend trip to their cottage. Henry blamed himself for their deaths as he had held up their departure for more than an hour. The bus he was coming home on after a school trip developed engine trouble. Being the loving son he was, he had phoned home to tell them of his predicament. Upon hearing the news, his father decided they could wait another sixty minutes for his return. If he wasn't home by then, they would go for the weekend without him. When he finally arrived home, the only people awaiting his arrival were two county police officers. If only he had phoned a few minutes, even a few seconds, earlier, they would have avoided being killed he thought. Since that fateful day, Henry had still not forgiven himself. Tina knew that now was the time for his healing process to begin.

"They send their love," she said quietly. She had never knowingly lied to Henry and she began to choke back her own tears as the words slipped from her lips.

"You saw them?"

"They were there to greet me."

Tears now began to form in Henry's eyes. He shook his head as memories long since forgotten of his youth streamed into his consciousness. "Do they blame me?" he cried.

"No, Henry. No." If Tina could have been granted one wish it would have been to hold Henry right then and there. Watching him collapse into sobs of anguish only a few inches away made her feel as helpless as Henry had as she lay dying in his arms. "They love you very much, Henry. They told me so." The words seemed to comfort and calm him. "I could tell from the way they spoke that you were one of the bright spots in their lives down here. And I could tell by your mother's expression that she would do almost anything to hold you again. Just as I would."

"Are you sure they were my parents you were talking to?"

"I'm positive."

"Well tell them that I miss them very much," Henry said, his voice crackling with emotion. "And that I love them." He looked into the eyes he had trusted all his life. "Will you please do that for me, Tina?"

"I'd be happy to."

Henry and Tina stood (and floated) in silence - both reflecting on their lives together and apart. As Henry brushed a tear from his cheek, he noticed something very curious: Tina's gown now swayed with the rhythm of the curtains.

"Tina - your dress!" he exclaimed. "It's moving! Does this mean you can stay here with me?" he asked excitedly.

"No, Henry," Tina replied gravely. "It means I have to go."

"But what about your dress? Why is it moving like that?" Tina had no explanation for it. "Well you can't just leave. Please stay just a little longer, will you?" Henry pleaded. "There is so much we still have to talk about."

The aura, that mystically surrounded Tina's body, appeared to glow slightly brighter, which sent a wave of panic through Henry's mind.

"We were together for fifty years, Henry," Tina said soothingly, as she noticed his anxiety. "And there are only three words over that entire space of time that really matter now." The tears that began to roll down Henry's face were contagious. Through her own watery eyes, Tina tried to say goodbye to the only man she had ever loved. "And if I could live my life over again, Henry, there's not one moment I would change. Or a single minute I would give away. With you, life was always a wonderful adventure." Tina placed her hands over Henry's quivering fingers, touching his wedding ring. "I never once regretted saying 'I do' to you."

Henry could feel her touch, but he knew she

was also slowly fading from him.

"And I loved you more than any person in this whole world, Tina. You were my world. I can't stand to see you leave me again."

"I'm not leaving," Tina said shaking her head. "I promised you before and I'll promise you again - I'll always be near you."

Tina leaned forward and kissed Henry's trembling lips for the last time, before slowly vanishing from sight.

"I love you, Tina," Henry whispered.

"And I love you."

Her voice seemed distant but Henry felt assured she was now in loving, caring hands. Feeling the breeze make its way into the room again, Henry went to the window to close it. As he did so he was astonished to see that the white carnation Tina had been holding lay on the sill.

Picking the delicate flower up, he brought it to his nose and inhaled its heavenly bouquet.

"Thank you, Tina," he said looking over at her picture. "I'll treasure this carnation as much as I treasured your company for all of these years."

Henry quickly shut the window and slid back into bed, placing the carnation on his night table.

"I always thought you were an angel, Tina," he said with a smile. "Now I know you are. Good night and sweet dreams."

In the morning Henry awoke to the fragrance of carnations. The night's events hadn't been a dream as he at first feared. As he got up he noticed the window was once again half opened. Instead of shutting it, he merely walked out of the room, confident in the knowledge that his loving wife had watched over him as he slept. She had promised she would always be near. As usual, she was as good as her word.

John R. Schlarbaum

Reviews are in...

THE DOCTOR'S BAG
A Sentimental Journey
by John Schlarbaum

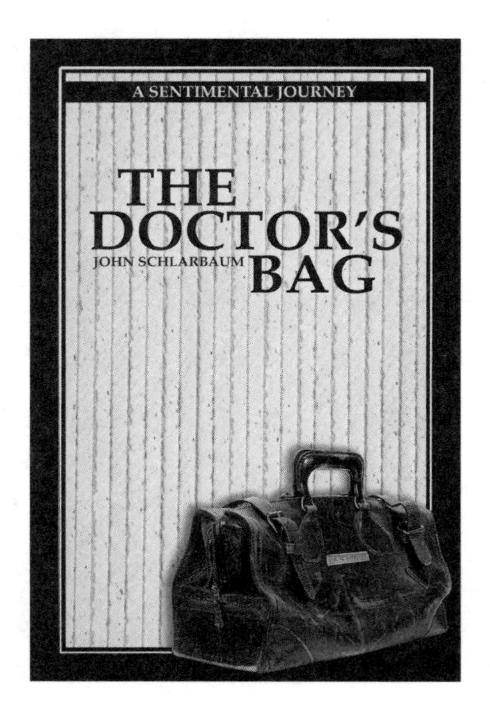

"I really enjoyed the book. It is honestly a tearjerker. It's very sentimental, very heartwarming, a really nice book. It would really make an excellent gift for someone."

TOM PARTINGTON, THE BOOK REVIEW, CKLW RADIO

"The Doctor's Bag is a book about life! As I walked through those pages I could relate so well to the ups and downs of 'family' sometimes as the child . . . other times as the parent. Well done! Thank you for your refreshing, inspirational message. Our world needs that."

JACKIE McCREARY, Windsor, Ontario

"The book was very good and I enjoyed it very much. I like that it was the father teaching the son life lessons through the bag. I especially liked the letter that the son finds from the father - it was beautifully written."

REBECCA PUDSEY, London, Ontario

"Just wanted to let you know how much I enjoyed your book, The Doctor's Bag. It was a very heartwarming, feel good story that made me laugh and cry. I will recommend it to all my family and friends."

CHERE MacNEILL , Burlington, Ontario

"How delightful it was to receive your book. I have just spent a most pleasurable time reading. You have penned a good tale – there is a message there too. I liked how you brought everything together at the end. The theme is universal but how uniquely you wove the generations into the story. I was touched in the closing with the emotion that came out."

GERREE BEACOM, West Lorne, Ontario

"I enjoyed your book. It was a fine story and the book now sits on the table in our family room."

DR. BRUCE CANTELON, West Lorne, Ontario

"I just wanted to let you know how much we enjoyed your book. What a wonderful read. We look forward to your next book. Best Wishes."

PETER AND KELLY ANDARY, Warren, Michigan, USA

"I have read your book and loved it. I typically read Classics and history books and truly your book brought a beautiful blend. It is an excellent book and I have passed it along to others to read."

MEL WELSHMAN, Burlington, Ontario

"I found the book very hard to put down because I really did want to find out what was going to happen next. It made me think about things and events in my own life parallel to the book and is a good story that makes you feel good in the end. I did really enjoy the book and will keep telling everyone about it."

JULIE LAWLEY, West Lorne, Ontario

"Wonderful story! I bought it yesterday and read it last night. Keep up the good work!"

DENISE NODDIN, Dutton, Ontario

If you have comments or want
to submit your own personal
READER'S REVIEW for

Aging Gracefully Together

Contact John at:
john@scannerpublishing.com

He would love to hear from you.

To purchase additional copies visit:
www.scannerpublishing.com

ABOUT THE AUTHOR:

John Schlarbaum was raised in the small town of West Lorne, Ontario. He began his professional writing career while working as a Writer and Field Director for several nationally syndicated Canadian television programs. These days he writes non-fiction reports in his career as a Private Investigator and is currently writing his next book.

His first book, ***The Doctor's Bag – A Sentimental Journey,*** which he'd written for his father, was well received when released in 2005.

Aging Gracefully Together – A Story of Love & Marriage was written as a special wedding gift for his friend, Sam Kirschner, on the occasion of his marriage to Sherry-Lynne Doucette.

The Past is the past.

The Future is now.

Everyday is a wonderful
new adventure.

Share it with someone
you love.

- John Schlarbaum